Sharkmaia
Adventures

The Last Guardian of the Ocean

I hope you think it's Fih-tastic! Katrina

KATRINA BARTON

THE CHOIR PRESS

First published in the United Kingdom in 2019 by
The Choir Press

ISBN 978-1-78963-038-1

Author's Note

I have done my best to research the ocean dwellers habits and habitats, and keep factual accuracies of this incredible world as much as possible. However, I have taken a few liberties. Of note are the locations of characters, particularly the two the main characters, Jack and Emily, a tiger-snout seahorse and a hawksbill turtle, who are able to swim freely about the ocean and live wherever Sabine lives. I have also taken liberty with some features and qualities of the sea creatures and made up certain personality traits for the purpose of characterisation, story and plot. My aim is to educate and inform while telling a lively and engaging story. The sea spiders I thought I had made up, until my proof-readers pointed out that they do indeed exist! Other than the name, these sea spiders are entirely a product of my imagination. I apologise for any issues the free rein of my storytelling may invoke. Please do feel free to contact me through my website www.sharkmaid.co.uk, with your thoughts or corrections. I would also like to note that I have continued to tinker after the final proofread was completed. All grammatical mistakes are therefore my own.

Lastly, while I have taken much pleasure from naming characters after friends and family, all characteristics are made up and therefore any likeness is entirely coincidental.

Acknowledgements

I cannot thank my cheerleaders enough, and there are a number of people I'd like to give a shout-out to:

My mother and father for telling me to go and do anything I wanted, and for always providing the financial support to enable me to follow this advice.

My sister, Susanna, and her husband, Andrew, who can be counted on for honest and unconditional support.

My close friends Lila Tahri-Morrison, Gareth Lewis and Samantha Davies for loving Sabine from the start, as well as for the brainstorming-over-wine sessions and the endless encouragement. That she exists is, in a large part, down to you guys.

Jo and Lizzie at Crescent Copywriting, who read as I wrote. Their encouragement and constant positive feedback kept me going on the marathon that completing a story can be.

Ben Cuffin-Munday, the very first reader when Sabine was barely a fully formed fishgirl. Ben contributed the vital information that octopus beaks (i.e. mouths) are not where I thought they were!

My later readers for their time and thoughts: Caitlin Evans, Ben McLaughlan, Christa Barton, Julia Quirk and Sophie Jenkins.

And to Garvin Thorp – the American who corrected my English. Time and time again.

Oh, and one more . . . a long-ago babysitter who let me watch *Jaws* when I should've been in bed . . .

To the real Jack and Emily

Contents

In Hawaiian folklore sharks are known as 'mano', meaning guardian and protector ...

Chapter One

A Chance Encounter

The beginning of the end began with a chance encounter.

Sabine's triangular fin glided through the surface of the water – a pale grey blade outlined with black markings and two small notches. Jack and Emily watched her fin moving towards them, sticking up high into the air. Sabine's head suddenly appeared, bobbing up and out of the water. She looked over to Jack and Emily and grinned wickedly. Then, with one slender arm, she threw their ball high into the air and smashed it over the net towards them.

Jack leapt up and knocked the ball back to her with his horse-shaped head. The momentum rolled him forwards and he somersaulted, landing back into the water with a flourish. Emily cheered and Sabine was so impressed that she missed the ball and it sailed right past her.

'Goal!' Sabine called out as Jack resurfaced and bounced up and down in victory.

'We win!' Emily yelled, turning to Jack and raising her flipper so that he could high-five her with his own, much smaller, fin. Sabine smiled to herself and leant back, floating in the cool water and letting it swirl over her stomach. She breathed in the fresh, salty air. It was a calm and lazy day off the southern coast of Spain; the sun peeked through wafts of drifting cloud and caught the tips of Sabine's fins, twinkling and sparkling upon the bluey-green water. As it was a perfect day for practising water volleyball, the three friends had stretched a net stitched out of seaweed across the surface of the water, the ends weighed down with seashells. They had spent the first part of the morning swimming up to it and throwing themselves over in a variety of leaps and twirls, or, in Emily's case, flinging herself over in less graceful moves. Her turtle shell was a stunning patchwork quilt of shapes and colours. The shell was a fortress and a home, but it was not much good when you wanted to dance around with your friends. After that, they had played a few rounds of water volleyball until they were exhausted.

'Shall we play something else?' Jack asked. His little orange fins were aching from all of the leaping around.

Their strawberry anemone-ball floated a little way off, gently moving with the water. Sabine ran her fingers over the rough grooves of her tail; then, swishing it from side to side, she swam over to get their ball.

'How about finball?' Emily said, suggesting her favourite game of knocking a ball around towards coral hoops while the other team tries to stop you.

'We really need another sea friend to play that,' Sabine replied, swimming over to them.

'Hide and seek?' Jack asked.

'No,' Emily moaned. 'It always takes me so long to find you two.'

2

'Then you need to practise!' Jack said.

'I could practise all day but I still wouldn't be able to change my colours and camouflage myself like you two can!' Emily wailed, before nodding reluctantly.

Jack grabbed his rucksack from where it was hanging on the seaweed net, pulled out his favourite stripy waistcoat and put it on. Sabine rolled the net up and placed it with their anemone-ball at the bottom of Jack's rucksack. Jack then huddled up into Sabine's hair next to one of her triangular, fin-shaped ears and wrapped his tail fin around a few strands of her locks so that he wouldn't drift away. He wasn't a very strong swimmer and felt safer being anchored to Sabine. Emily took a gulp of air and snapped the bracelet on her right flipper to the bracelet on Sabine's left wrist. Sabine and Emily wore matching bracelets made out of freshwater pearls in blue and green colours surrounding a square magnetic bead in the centre.

The two bracelets clicked into place by their magnets, attaching Emily to Sabine. Emily and Jack can't swim as fast as Sabine, so they have to hitch a ride if they want to keep up.

Together, they sank down into the ocean. Sabine felt the water close over the top of her head, her brown hair floating up as if coming to life. The

3

water pressed in around her and she
breathed in through the gills on either side of
her neck. The land in the distance changed
colour from greens and browns to softer,
darker shades under the water.

Sabine suddenly tapped Emily's shell and
said, 'You're it!' Then she turned and raced away. Jack hot-
hopped on his tail after Sabine. Emily sighed and covered
her eyes with her flippers and began counting. They were
both going to be hard to find. Sabine was able to
camouflage herself against objects and take on the colours of
her surroundings; it's something that seahorses are good at
too. Jack is a bright-orange tiger
snout seahorse and he can
camouflage himself fantastically,
blending in with the sea flowers
around him. He had found it a

very handy skill when guarding against danger. But Emily
had an idea. She finished counting to 50 and then crept over
to the nearest bright coral ledge, knowing that Jack wouldn't
have been able to get too far. A variety of fish swam
dreamily and calmly, in and out of the rock formation. There
were orange fish with vertical blue stripes, yellow fish with
horizontal green stripes and purple fish with orange spots
dotted all over them. In amongst the blue and green fronds,
a rim of rock was sticking out, upon which a fiery red coral
had grown. Emily sneaked up and reached out her flipper.
She ran the tip gently along one of the branches. Nothing
stirred. She moved onto another branch and repeated the
action. No movement. Onto the
next one. Emily gently flicked
her fin over it. It twitched
slightly. She ran her flipper
up and down, tickling the
branch. Suddenly, the
branch chuckled, coming to
life, and two black eyes
opened as an arched head leaned
forward, choking on its own giggles.

5

Jack yelled, 'That's not fair, Emily!'

Emily did a backflip in victory.

'Hurray,' she sang and then looked over at Jack. She knew he hated to lose but he smiled, trying to be a good sport. Jack joined Emily to look for Sabine. They swam around, carefully staring at every flower and every rock, trying to find Sabine's shape in any of them. Emily and Jack rounded a large chunk of volcanic rock and were surprised to see Sabine hovering, finning the water waiting for them. They went over and joined her.

'Sabine?' Emily asked.

Sabine turned and looked at them in excitement. 'There's a rip current over there. Can you feel it pulling us?'

'Oh wow,' said Jack, and they swam over to the narrow band of water where a strong current had built up, and they all jumped in. They were immediately swept along as if on a water slide! Sabine kicked her tail to go faster and zipped off ahead of them. Jack was buffeted

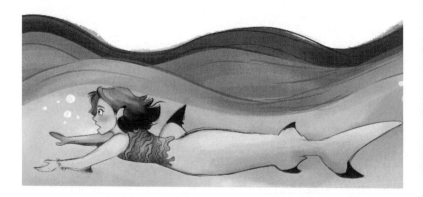

from side to side and leaned his little body into the current, uncurling his tail as if surfing underwater. Emily spread her flippers wide and drifted along. A tear in her left flipper from where it had been caught in the plastic rings of a pack of coke cans meant that Emily had to work harder to navigate to stay on course, but she had become extremely skilled at spinning. Using her back flippers to steer, she could spin around and around in circles, always returning to Sabine – like a boomerang!

They laughed and called out to each other, until finally the rip current ended and they were thrown out into the deep ocean. Jack and Emily were still giggling and feeling giddy when they noticed that Sabine had stopped and was staring up at something. They swam over and floated next to her. In front of them, stretching away above and below and reaching out to the left and right, was a ginormous net. Strands of rope had been knitted together and criss-crossed over each other to form small square holes. Dank water

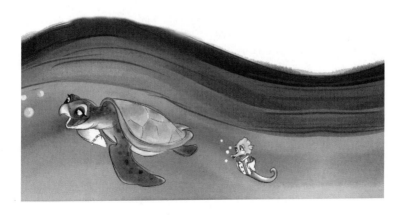

seeped like a mist towards them carrying the stale smell of rotting flesh.

'What is that?' Jack asked.

'That must be the net The Kilk put up,' Emily answered.

'It's *The Dark Wave*,' Sabine said and Jack propelled himself into her hair and the three hung suspended, staring through the net in silence. Five years ago, a sea demon called The Kilk had put up a net between the southern tip of Spain and the northern tip of Morocco to catch and kill sharks in the Mediterranean Sea. He believed that sharks were incredibly powerful and so he was killing them for use in his staff – a large, spear-like weapon. The sea creatures caught inside could not leave, and, without the natural flow of them freely migrating back and forth, the ocean there had become dark and lifeless.

'Sabine?' A small voice suddenly called her name and the three turned in surprise to see a little fish zigzagging her way through the water towards them. Sabine kicked her tail and swam closer to her, but, as she slowly came into focus, Sabine realised that she didn't recognise her.

'I don't believe it,' the little fish

said, gazing at Sabine. Sabine looked at her, taking in her vivid purple-green colours, which lit up the ocean, shining like the beacon from a lighthouse. She was a stunning unicorn tang fish.

'What are you doing here? I thought you were on the other side of the world,' the unicorn tang fish said.

'We were, but we're exploring,' Sabine replied carefully, feeling very freaked out that this fish seemed so familiar with her.

'It's so good to see you,' the fish said.

'What's your name?' Sabine asked.

The fish seemed seashell-shocked and stared up at her. 'It's me, Lila!'

Emily and Jack came up behind Sabine.

'This is Jack and Emily,' Sabine said, nodding to the bright-orange seahorse and the brown-patterned turtle. Emily waved, and Jack bowed politely before taking the opportunity to break away. He stuffed his head inside his rucksack and started slurping down some shrimps. Seahorses have no stomachs, so Jack eats up to 50 meals a day. Emily rolled her eyes at him and tried to grab a few morsels out of his bag, but Jack was expecting this and was too quick for her – he ducked away, still slurping.

'And I'm Sabine,' Sabine said, somewhat pointlessly. 'Is this *The Dark Wave*?' she asked Lila, gesturing to the net behind them.

Lila blinked at her a few times in surprise before answering, 'Yes. I'm on my way to visit Tanner. He's recently escaped.'

'Who's Tanner?' Sabine asked.

'He's … he's a stingray …' Lila stuttered out.

Jack, with his head still inside his rucksack, involuntarily shuddered as seahorses often find themselves on the menu for stingrays.

'… who got caught up in *The Dark Wave*,' Lila continued.

Sabine froze. Jack pulled his head out of his rucksack. Emily gulped.

'He was kidnapped by The Kilk,' Lila said cautiously, her eyes fixed intently on Sabine.

Emily put a flipper to her mouth at the horror of it. 'That's awful,' she said.

'He's doing ok, but he spends all his time on his own now and we think he's agoraphobic,' Lila said.

'What's agoraphobic?' Jack asked.

'It's when you're cave-stuck,' Emily answered, 'and are too scared to go outside.'

Sabine felt a cold sickness creep into the pit of her belly, right where her torso melts into her shark's body and tail. 'Oh, how terrifying,' she said.

'Tanner's building a whole network of tunnels for himself out of the coral,' Lila continued, 'and he just stays in there. He's even got a guard outside who fetches his food for him.'

'How did he escape?' Emily asked.

'He taught himself to fly … like a Mobula ray, and he flew over the net,' Lila answered.

'It's awful what is going on in *The Dark Wave*,' Sabine whispered.

'Yeah, I really need to get going and see how he's doing,' Lila said.

'If he's cave-stuck, it's not like he's going anywhere . . .' Jack couldn't help himself, mumbling through a mouthful of plankton, but Sabine caught Lila's shocked reaction and threw him a look of caution.

'Can you blame him?' Lila glared. 'And where were you when all this was going on?'

'What do you . . .' Jack said, but he trailed off and acknowledged Sabine's look with an apologetic shrug.

'I'd better get going,' Lila said. 'I've still got half a day of steady swimming to reach Tanner.' She took another long look at Sabine and then waved at them with a sad smile. 'It was good to see you,' she said. Then she turned and swam off, leaving the trio watching her, completely confused by this exchange.

'Let's head home,' Sabine said, and, with a last look at the shark net, they fastened themselves together and headed north, back to the southern coast of Spain.

A few fin lengths away, hiding behind a rock, Lila watched Sabine's grey tail with its black smudges around the edges disappear through the murkiness, heading in the direction of clearer water. Sabine is one of a kind: she has arms, hands, shoulders and a sweet face with an upturned button nose surrounded by shoulder-length dark hair. She also has the tail of a blacktip reef shark. There used to be other sharkmaids like her in the ocean, but Sabine does not remember that she has forgotten them. Lila made up her mind and swam off in a different direction. There was now another stingray she needed to see much more urgently than Tanner ...

Chapter Two

A Cavern of Stingrays

Amongst the bumpy ridges of a small, cavernous outcrop, Sabine, Jack and Emily were asleep. Pressed into the shadows, Sabine was curled up, her fins folded comfortably into the naturally occurring grooves of a brown boulder of rock, her tail wrapped around her like a blanket. Jack lolled back and forth, anchored into place by his tail, which was wrapped around a bright-red, twig-like coral branch, each breath in sending him rolling forwards and each breath out sending him rolling backwards. The sleeves of his green-and-red-striped pyjamas dragged back and forth through the water with his rhythm. Emily lay flat out, higher up on a lip of rock, covered with a mattress of moss-like sponges and seaweed, one flipper covering her eyes like an eye mask. Like other turtles, Emily can hold her breath for a few hours, but then she needs to pop up to the surface and breathe, so her bed was the closest to the entrance. Strands of dark-green seaweed hung down over the large opening swinging with the current and enclosing the chamber. Each morning, sunlight sparkled in between the strands, announcing the new day. Little else was in the cave, except for Jack's collection of striped waistcoats and jumpers and his rucksack filled with food and anemone-balls.

As Jack snored away on his perch, a sudden resistance in the water stopped him from tipping forward and caused him instead to pitch a little too far backwards. He twitched uncomfortably but continued melodically swaying, lost in his dreams. But then ... there it was again. A movement in the water – a strange sense of something right in front of him. He jerked awake suddenly, shaking his head and slowly bringing the world into focus. In front of him, staring straight into his face, was a set of floating eyes: two small black dots seemingly suspended by themselves in the dimness of the cavern. Jack tensed and straightened up, words escaping his mouth in short beats.

'Sab ... Sabi ... Sabine!'

Sabine fidgeted deep in a dream world of her own.

'Sabine!' Jack raised the volume of his cries until she finally jolted awake. She uncurled herself and sat up. As she rubbed her eyes, slowly coming to, she saw that their whole home was filled with dark floating creatures. She shot up off her rock and hung, finning the water back and forth with her tail, and looking at all of the pairs of eyes focusing on her. Jack uncurled his tail and backed away from the floating eyes staring straight into his. Once he'd got a few precious inches between them, he saw that they were attached to a flat, two-dimensional creature that seemed to hover like a kite. He circled his eyes in his head and looked around, frightened, taking in the number of suspended stingrays.

There were Atlantic torpedo stingrays, smalleye stingrays, bullnose stingrays ... 20, maybe 30, floating on top of each other, pushing and shoving, jostling for space, crammed inside the coral skeleton cavern.

'What's going on?' Sabine looked towards the seaweed drapes, trying to guess what time it might be by the weak light seeping through the dangling strands. The stingrays were blocking the entrance, making it very hard to tell if it was still night-time. Sabine looked to Jack, who quickly bobbed over to her. He was not scared of rays when he was with her, but he was certainly nervous with so many suddenly showing up in his home. He knew that, in other circumstances, he would be a happy addition to their dinner plate! Emily shifted, still sleeping deeply, her fins doing a good job of shielding her from the noise.

Sabine looked around, making eye contact with each of the different rays and becoming aware of the waves of electricity that they gave off. Sabine has the same holes around her nose that sharks and rays have – a sixth sense that picks up electrical currents given off by other fish and sea creatures. Electricity carries well through water, especially salty water, so Sabine can sense movement and find fish that are very far away.

'Well?' Sabine said.

No one answered and finally she placed her hands on her

hips at the point where her pinkish-grey skin turns into rough, denticles, the hard, tooth-like structures of shark skin. She stared directly at the closest ray, refusing to look away until he spoke. He was a cownose stingray – a pale creature with a broad face, rounded nose and wide-set eyes. He seemed to be the one in charge and he stared openly back at Sabine. The silence edged on and Sabine pressed her lips together and raised her eyebrows. Finally, he spoke. He had a high-pitched voice that seemed to boomerang off the walls around them.

'Sabine. We do apologise for invading your home at such an hour, but we have travelled from afar to speak with you on a matter of grave importance,' the cownose stingray said.

Sabine frowned and Jack pulled his chin back into his chest and made a face, suggesting how over-the-top he thought this stingray was.

'We heard that you were here and I must say that we were thrilled. You cannot imagine the distance we have covered in the last five years searching for you.'

'Searching for us?' Sabine repeated.

'For five years?' Jack repeated.

'You, Sabine, not your tiny horse friend.' He focused entirely on Sabine, ignoring Jack.

Jack's eyes narrowed and he went to speak, but Sabine quickly talked over him, 'Who told you that we were here?'

'Lila informed us,' the stingray answered.

'And why me?' Sabine asked.

'We need your help. Help that only you can give,' the stingray said.

'Who are you?' Sabine snapped, starting to feel irritated.

He sighed dramatically and said, 'My name is Sir Raynault.'

'Hmmm ...' Jack's cheeks puffed out as he tried to suppress a laugh and he slowly let out his breath with a smirk.

'I am in charge of the Messenger Rays,' Sir Raynault said proudly.

This was met by blank expressions from both Sabine and Jack. Two of the rays started whispering urgently to each other and the chatter started up amongst the other rays filling the cavern.

'Quiet!' Sir Raynault snapped, twisting his whole body around to glare at them.

The noise finally disturbed Emily. One of her flippers twitched and slipped from her face. The whole cavern of creatures went silent as they watched her. She moved her other flipper off her eyes, shuddered and stretched, opening one bleary eye.

'Whaaa?' Emily frowned, finding her way from semi-consciousness to consciousness, and then she was up, spinning into position next to Sabine's right pectoral fin.

The trio now floated in an arrow formation, facing the army of rays, Sabine at the helm.

'The Sea Council is meeting tomorrow and they have requested that you attend,' Sir Raynault said.

'Who are the Messenger Rays?' Sabine asked.

17

'We were the group of rays that ran Scalewave before The Kilk tricked Tanner and took over the Mediterranean Sea,' Sir Raynault answered.

'I don't know why you think we can help,' Sabine said.

'We are gathering the masses, planning an uprising, putting together a movement, forming ...'

'We get the point,' Jack cut him off.

'It's time to face what is happening over in the next ocean. We need to swim together, fin to fin, to face the enemy,' Sir Raynault said passionately.

Sabine looked at Jack and Emily, taking in what they thought. Jack shook his head softly at what sounded very much like a lot of danger.

Emily was still half asleep, but she looked to Sabine and said, 'Have you ever heard of Scalewave?'

Sabine shook her head as another stingray pushed past Sir Raynault, clearly thinking that enough was enough.

'Henry is in trouble,' she said. This stingray was about a third of the size of the others. She was small, a teenager, and yet she wore a fierce expression and had determination in her oil-black eyes.

'Henry?' Jack asked.

'Henry Hammerhead,' Sabine said flatly.

'Who are you?' Emily asked her.

The stingray nodded at Sabine and answered Emily, 'I'm Toyah. A close friend of Ava's.'

Sabine drew in her breath and let it out slowly. Ava was Henry's angel fish and his best friend.

'You can help, Sabine,' Toyah said.

'But I can only camouflage,' Sabine said, frowning at her.

'Toyah,' Sir Raynault interrupted. 'Stand down.'

He turned to Sabine, 'The more sea folk we can get together and form a plan with, the better our chances of success. The Sea Council requests that you attend our meeting tomorrow. Henry is just the latest shark to be caught in the shark net The Kilk set up.'

'He's completely tangled up in it and we can't break him out,' Toyah spoke up again. Sir Raynault sent her a stern look to quieten her, but Toyah didn't seem scared by it and carried on. 'Someone has to do something; he doesn't have long before he dies and The Kilk could appear at any time,' she said, her voice starting to rise.

'Come with us. We will travel to the meeting together,' Sir Raynault continued.

'I'm not sure,' Jack said, angling his body to Sabine and looking genuinely scared and more than a bit suspicious.

Suddenly, a few rays swam a couple of strokes forwards and hovered intimidatingly. Jack stretched out his tail and quickly beat the fins on his back to propel himself into Sabine's hair.

'The council is desperate,' Sir Raynault said, starting to plead.

'Of course we will come with you,' Sabine said, still confused but also rather curious about the request from the Sea Council. 'We want to help Henry in any way we can but please do not try and intimidate us.'

Sir Raynault bowed his head, which flipped the rest of his body up. 'Thank you, Miss Sabine,' he said.

Jack looked to Emily and they both sniggered and rolled their eyes.

'Let's go. We want to get to the meeting on time,' Sir Raynault said and turned to the other rays. They slowly started to filter out of the cavern. Jack sighed with relief and Emily relaxed as well now that there was more room to breathe.

Jack pulled off his pyjamas, put on his favourite green-and-yellow-striped jumper and started loading up his rucksack with other jumpers and waistcoats, making sure his food was neatly packed around them.

Sabine turned towards Emily and held out her wrist. Emily lifted up her flipper with the magnetic bead exposed and the two bracelets snapped together. They hovered, waiting for Jack to finish getting ready. They watched as he fussed with his things until Emily lost patience and said to Jack, exasperated, 'Jack, we need to go! Henry is in trouble. Stop faffing.'

'Stop fiddling,' Sabine said.

'Stop diddling.'

'Stop delaying.'

'Stop playing.'

'Stop ...' Sabine searched for the next rhyming word, '... neighing.'

Emily fell about laughing and wiped her eyes with her fins, while Jack gave them both a withering look, then joined in laughing at their silliness. He pulled his rucksack onto his back and skipped up Sabine's arm, wrapping his tail around strands of her hair to rest in his usual position on her right side near her fin-shaped ear. Sabine swam out of the cavern that had been their home for the last few weeks and followed the trail of stingrays. With Jack fixed into the folds of her locks and Emily pulled along by their connected bracelets, they made their way to the surface so Emily could easily pop up and breathe.

The night sky was bright, stars sprinkled across it lighting their way as they began the journey south. Sir Raynault had been hanging back, waiting for them. As they caught up to him, he turned in acknowledgement and they all swam along together.

'So, who knighted you as a sir?' Sabine asked, making conversation.

'Your father did,' he answered, looking straight ahead.

Sabine stopped swimming in shock and Jack and Emily exchanged surprised, wide-eyed glances, but Sir Raynault refused to look at her and swam on.

Chapter Three

The Sea Council

'Cetus is out,' Emily said to Sabine, looking up at the light that flickered down through the ocean. Sabine kicked her tail and, arching her head upwards, swam to the surface to take a break. Emily poked her neck out of the water and let out a big breath, sucking fresh air back in.

'That's not a good sign,' Jack said, looking up at Cetus – a cluster of stars making up a constellation that looks like a sea monster.

'It's a bad omen,' Emily agreed.

'It's an old fish-folk tale,' Sabine said, not bothered by it. Two of the stars shone brightly on either side of the sea monster – one marking its head and the other marking its tail. The rest of the stars glinted softly, filling in its body.

'I think we should take it as a warning and turn back,' Jack said.

Sabine laughed, 'Jack, we'll bear it in mind ok, but I believe a lot of luck is about attitude.' Jack frowned, not at all convinced that their attitude could save them.

Sabine lay back, floating on the surface and spreading her fingers out wide letting the water flow over them. After a few minutes of chilling, they ducked back down and carried on after the stingrays. Toyah was at the back of the group – a fever – and turned around every so often to make sure they were still there.

Finally, she called out to them, 'We're nearly there.'

Sabine sensed it before she saw it, the freckles on her face tingled. They were actually tiny holes that could send out electric waves and pick up even the faintest vibration given off from objects. Electrical currents bounced back to her, suggesting that directly ahead there was an object of considerable size. As the pulses came back stronger and more intense, Sabine sped up with excitement until they were staring up at the Dialis, which was a huge flower-shaped structure made out of layers and layers of wide coral pieces shaped like leaves.

There was no stalk, but just a thick flower head that seemed to grow up and out of the sandy seabed. They swam up the outside and over the top to look down into the centre. The large, leaf-shaped pieces were crinkly and knobbly and looked like they could be easily crushed, but were actually solid structures and very comfortable to rest on. They had been placed on top of each other, fanning outwards and upwards like petals, creating a large flower. Each section contained its own tiered seating, like a football stadium or concert hall. The enormous size of it meant that many fish could attend the social events or meetings that were held here.

In the middle, as if the bud of the flower, a raised podium had been carved out of the sand. A large upturned seashell was set upon it, around which an assortment of creatures were deep in conversation. At the end of the seashell, a large

24

piece of black slate was propped up against a makeshift stand build out of miniature seashells and held together with seaweed and sand.

Sabine took in the scene. A striped eel catfish sat at the head of the group. The whiskers that give catfish their name sprouted from underneath his mouth, giving him the appearance of a wise old man. Long white stripes ran down his thin, black body to his fins, which were fused together much like how the fins on eels are. Next to him there was an amazing halfmoon doubletail betta fish, a plumage of fins spread out around her like a peacock's feathers. In an array of colours, the tail extended upwards and outwards nearly tripling her size. On the other side of the catfish was a zebra moray eel. These beautiful creatures are striped with black and yellowish-white rings along the length of their bodies just like zebras. Eels can look very scary with their long, snake-like bodies, but they are fascinating creatures. Instead of having scales the ooze a slimy substance to protect against parasites and cuts and scrapes. To the right of the betta fish, there was another stunning fish: a painted greenling. She was a soft brown colour with rough splashes of red running down her body, as if made by a shaky fin holding a paintbrush. Sir Raynault and the rays swam halfway down and then paused, waiting and watching while Sabine, Jack and Emily took seats at the back. Toyah came over and sat next to them.

The catfish looked around the members of the council and called the meeting to order.

'The agenda for today …' He paused and turned to his assistant, a young yellow-ribboned sweetlips fish nervously balancing a pile of sea scrolls in his fins. He bumbled about; then, seeming to have lost something, he panicked and dropped the scrolls.

He picked them up and started flapping, sorting through them. The assembled sea creatures waited patiently as he shuffled papers, coughed nervously, then made his way around each attendant handing out copies of the meeting's agenda. As each creature scanned down the list of items on the scroll, the young fish picked up a shell with a bony, pen-like point at the end and took his place next to the slate.

No one spoke. Finally, the little fish looked over to the catfish, who was staring silently at him, waiting for the little fish to notice his disapproval.

'Thank you, Howard. A quick run through the list . . .' The catfish turned his attention back to the group. Then, realising someone was missing, he said, 'Where's Eli?'

No one responded.

'The dolphins aren't here yet either, Gibbons,' the stunning betta fish piped up.

'We can cope without them, Almu,' Gibbons said.
'Where's Eli?' he said again. And again, no one spoke.

Finally, deciding to move on, Gibbons looked down at his sea scroll and the other fish followed suit.

'The agenda for today is . . .'

<u>Agenda for the Sea Council:</u>
- The increase of plastic in the East Pacific
- The kidnapping of seahorses by Land Creatures
- The rise of fin rot disease in young fish
- The destruction of The Kilk

On the reading of the last item, all the creatures looked to each other nervously.

At that moment, two dolphins wearing sunglasses and over-the-top, colourful Hawaiian shirts appeared over the top of the Dialis and rested, unseen, upon the back benches. One of the dolphins noticed Sabine and, nudging his friend, swam over.

'Sabine?' he asked curiously.

She nodded.

'This is Marvin,' the dolphin said and held out a flipper, gesturing towards his friend.

'And this is Garvin,' the other dolphin said, joining him and pointing his own flipper back at Garvin.

'Garvin?' Jack asked.

'Like Gavin,' Marvin said.

'Or Marvin,' Garvin said.

'Nice to meet you Marvin and Garvin,' Sabine held out a hand and, in turn, they each slapped the front of their fin to the palm of Sabine's hand and then back across the back of her hand with the back of their fin.

'...and this is Jack and Emily,' she continued.

'Ah, then we shall call you J-EM!' Garvin said, connecting their names.

'Clever!' Emily said. 'I like it.'

The group chatted easily, whilst back on the floor, the meeting continued.

'The oceans are rising. We need to address this first,' Almu said.

'It's not on the list,' Gibbons said.

'It's important!' Almu said, 'I put it on the list last time.'

'There are many important issues,' Gibbons said. 'We can only address so much at each meeting.'

Almu crossed her fins over and huffed.

'Let's have a vote on whether to include this topic,' Gibbons said.

'We can't vote. There is no representative for the octopuses today,' the eel pointed out.

'Then let's move on,' Gibbons said.

'We should vote,' Almu insisted.

'No, I agree with Finn,' Gibbons said.

'If they are not here to vote on a topic that I want to discuss now, it won't matter to them if we discuss it!' Almu protested.

Marvin and Garvin decided that this was the time to make their grand entrance and they started talking as they came forwards, interrupting proceedings. They were the infamous double act of the Sea Council.

'No-shows get no vote, I say.'

'So, they lose out, I say.'

'Let's vote on it without them, I say.'

'You're both talking but saying very little,' Gibbons said, looking up at the crazily dressed dolphins as they swam down towards the group and took their places around the table. Gibbons pressed his lips together and narrowed his eyes at them.

'Thanks for coming,' Finn said as he glared at them.

'You two want a say?' the painted greenling said.

'We're council members, Maddy,' Marvin grinned at her.

'Only because the spinner dolphins voted you on as a joke,' Almu said.

'A vote's a vote. When they vote and you win the vote, you're voted.' Garvin said.

'Huh?' Almu stared at him.

'Don't call me Maddy,' the painted greenling, Madison, said.

'No, we wait until next month to vote on when we discuss this topic,' Gibbons said to shut down the conversation. 'We need Eli.'

'Who is Eli?' Jack whispered to Sabine.

Toyah leaned in and said, 'He's an octopus. Widely respected.'

'Wait here,' Sir Raynault called back to them and then swam down to the centre of the Dialis.

'We found her,' he said as he approached the group. 'Sabine is here.'

'Fantastic!' Almu exclaimed. 'Get her down here now.'

'No,' Gibbons interrupted. 'Let's wait for Eli to get here.'

'We're out of time,' Finn agreed, backing up Almu.

'We've been waiting too long for this,' Almu said. 'She could be the key to end this.'

Gibbons sighed and nodded, rubbing a fin up and down over his forehead.

'So why don't we ask her?' Garvin said and they all turned to follow his gaze.

'At last,' Finn said as Sabine swam up to them and stopped next to him.

Chapter Four

Henry the Hammerhead Shark

Gibbons gestured to the seat directly opposite him at the other end of the upturned seashell. Sabine took a deep breath in and swam over the bumpy, petal-shaped seating, down into the centre of the Dialis. She took a seat at the tail end of the table, Jack and Emily trailed behind and came to a stop, hovering on either side of her shoulders. There was an awkward silence, everyone seemed to just want to look at her and Sabine didn't understand why. As the only sharkmaid in the ocean, she knew she was unique, but she was starting to feel like she'd been captured by a Land Creature and put into an aquarium. Up close, Sabine could see them all more clearly. They had kindly faces, and Finn and Madison looked at her with wide open smiles. Almu, however, stared hard at Sabine. Jack glared back at Almu. Emily ran her eyes around the group. Sabine smiled nervously. Howard coughed.

Then Madison spoke. 'Thanks for coming, Sabine. We've asked ...'

'Eli should be here to explain,' Gibbons interrupted.

'No!' Almu looked exasperated. 'If he can't be bothered to show up, let alone be on time ...'

'He's only got seven tentacles! You know it takes him that bit longer to get anywhere.'

'Then he should have left earlier,' Almu argued.

'Why does he only have seven tentacles?' Sabine asked. More silence from the group.

Sabine frowned and then looked at Sir Raynault, 'What do you know about my father?'

'You mentioned her father?!' Finn asked and Sir Raynault quickly looked down at the seashell table and didn't answer.

'You really don't remember, do you?' Sir Raynault asked, his eyes flicked briefly towards Sabine then back down to the table.

'I told you she wouldn't,' Madison snapped at him.

'I thought she was pretending,' Sir Raynault said.

'Pretending? Not to remember ... *what*?' Sabine stared hard at Sir Raynault until he finally met her gaze.

'Not to remember how *The Dark Wave* started,' Sir Raynault said.

'You all just think she is ignoring it, playing all day with her friends, not caring. Well she doesn't remember and she can't remember,' Madison snapped.

Emily twisted her neck around to get a look at Sabine's face. Her expression showed both confusion and fear and Emily felt a rush to protect her.

'Tell us what is going on or we're leaving,' Emily said, looking around at each one of them.

'Ok,' Gibbons said and then snapped at Sir Raynault. 'Just tell her.'

'The sea demon, The Kilk ...' Sir Raynault began.

33

Sabine nodded. Jack shivered. Emily tucked her neck into her shell.

'Since The Kilk set up his net around the Mediterranean Sea, the number of sharks we're losing is rising to tens of thousands,' Sir Raynault said.

'And this is on top of the number of sharks the Land Creatures kill every year,' Finn said.

'He's stealing the cartilage from sharks,' Madison said, referring to the soft and flexible tissue that shark and stingray skeletons are made of.

'Why shark cartilage?' Sabine asked.

'Sharks are seen as godly, and The Kilk believes it strengthens his staff and makes him more powerful,' Gibbons told her.

'We cannot continue to stand by and do nothing,' Almu said. 'We'll have no sharks left!'

'What would that mean?' Jack asked.

'As top predators in the ocean, they help control the number of other creatures in the sea. Without them feeding, the other fish are growing and overeating, so the numbers of plants and algae are, in turn, becoming smaller. This reduces the oxygen in the ocean and now other fish can't breathe and are dying.' Alum explained.

'The delicate web of the ecosystem,' Emily said to herself.

'Tell her the plan,' Gibbons said.

'We are going to break through the net and into the Mediterranean Sea, bait The Kilk, attack him and steal his staff,' Finn said. 'Without that, he will be weakened and then we can kill him.'

'Oh, is that all?' Jack asked sarcastically.

'What will you use as bait?' Emily asked.

'A seahorse ...' Sir Raynault said.

Jack's eyes widened.

'Kidding,' Sir Raynault said.

Jack did not find this funny. Nor did Sabine.

'How do we come into this?' she demanded.

'Not we ... actually ... you ...' Finn said.

'So you DO want to use us as bait!' Sabine was angry.

'No,' Gibbons was quick to say. 'We need your help getting the staff.'

'You see, he is terrified of sharks because of their power and strength and that's why he wants them all dead,' Finn explained.

'And the sharks deserve to be rescued anyway,' Toyah had snuck up to the seashell table and cut in.

'So that's why you want me, because I am half shark?' Sabine asked.

'Well, more than that ...' Finn said, uncomfortable.

'We believe you are the key to end this,' Almu said.

'... bit dramatic,' Jack muttered.

'Tell me what it is I don't remember,' Sabine snapped, restless.

'Your father used to work protecting the oceans. He set up a system called Scalewave where stingrays would pick up on distressed fish and relay the message to each other across the ocean, back to your father, and then he would go and save them,' Finn explained.

'Wow,' said Jack. 'That's cool.'

Madison swam up off her seat and floated above the seashell table. 'He was training you to be next,' she said.

'This isn't true!' Sabine protested.

'He wanted you to protect the oceans with him,' Madison said gently.

'Why don't I remember him?' Sabine asked her.

'The Kilk set a trap . . .' Madison said gently.

'I don't believe you,' Sabine was shaking her head, not letting Madison finish.

Jack and Emily looked at each other, distressed.

'Sabine . . .' Madison tried to continue.

'No!' Sabine snapped not wanting to hear any more.

'Let's go to Eli's,' Finn suggested. 'He can help explain. We should check up on him anyway; it's unlike him not to be here.'

The rest of the council, excluding Almu, nodded in agreement.

'Ok, but not everyone,' Gibbons said. 'Just Finn and me.'

'And us,' said Marvin.

'No,' Gibbons said.

'Yes,' said Garvin.

'I'd like them to come,' Sabine said, turning to Gibbons. For some reason, the two dolphins with their similar names and matching Hawaiian shirts helped Sabine feel at ease. Marvin and Garvin grinned, and Gibbons nodded, exasperated.

Howard coughed and consulted his notes.

'He's about one third of a morning's swim north-east of here.'

Gibbons nodded. 'Great. Sir Raynault, you stay here with your team. The rest of us, let's go.'

Sir Raynault came forward, 'Why don't I go on ahead and let him know you're coming? I am a Messenger Ray after all.'

'Head Messenger Ray actually,' Toyah butted in once more.

'No,' said Gibbons. 'I think we should all stick together in our two groups. You stay here and check in with Lieutenant Howes.'

Sir Raynault turned away and swam over to his team to rest with his back to the Sea Council.

'Let's go,' Gibbons said.

The catfish, the eel, the two dolphins, Sabine, Jack and Emily swam up and over the Dialis and out into the vast ocean.

They swam along in a group, sticking closely together, and had barely covered any distance when Sabine stopped suddenly. She looked around in confusion, spinning on the spot.

'There's a fish in distress. I can feel it.'

'Sabine, come on,' Gibbons said, pausing briefly to look back at her. He carried on, but Sabine didn't move.

'No, I can feel it.' Sabine was certain. She could sense the electromagnetic currents pulsing through the salty water. A fish, large in size, was sending out weak signals – a sign of vulnerability.

Sabine turned and took a few strokes in that direction.

'It's Henry,' Garvin finally gave in. 'We know he's in distress; we told you. That's why we're doing this.'

'Come with us,' Marvin said. 'Let's go and talk to Eli and end this. Think of the bigger picture.'

But Sabine was fraught, 'No, Henry ... we need to go and save Henry!'

'Eli first,' Gibbons insisted.

But Sabine was not listening and she took off, Jack and Emily in tow.

'Sabine, come back!' Gibbons yelled, but she was already gone.

Sabine swam frantically towards the distress signal followed by the rest of the group, until she saw him up ahead. He was hard to miss. Completely entangled in the sea demon's shark net, Henry was twisted up from head to tail. Bound by the ropes, one half of his hammer-shaped head was sticking through the square mesh.

Henry was thrashing around trying to pull forward, but it was causing the ropes that bound him to cut deeper into his body. The eyes on either end of his unusual shaped head were darting around. He was looking at Sabine on one side of the net and, on the other side, he was looking deep into the Mediterranean Sea – where *The Dark Wave* was.

'Henry!' Sabine was horrified and hurried over to him, placing her hands around the side of Henry's head that stuck out towards her, trying to comfort him. Jack was speechless, shock washing through his small body as he took in the scene. A group of angel fish was buzzing around trying to comfort Henry but all feeling very helpless. Ava, Henry's best angel fish friend, was zig-zagging around him in a complete panic. Angel fish like Ava are very close to hammerhead sharks – even more so than their shark buddies. One is never far from the other, and Ava is never far from Henry, pecking in between his dermal scales and keeping him clean.

'He's drowning!' Ava cried out.

Sabine caught hold of Ava in her hand as she passed over Henry's head and gently stroked her, attempting to calm her down. Angel fish look small next to their shark friends, but in Sabine's hand she was actually quite big. Her body was a deep black colour, decorated with vibrant yellow fins.

'Ava, try and catch your breath. We'll help him, I promise!' Sabine told her.

Ava looked down into Sabine's palm and wept gently. Sabine handed her over to Emily, who held her in her flippers and made soothing noises.

Sabine turned to Henry and said, 'Henry, stop trying to move,' but she knew that Henry must try and keep moving in order to pump water over his gills to get oxygen. Some sharks can breathe while staying still, but not Henry. Hammerheads need the swimming motion to draw water into their gills. Yet every knot was made worse by his frantic thrashing in his panic to breathe.

'You have to try and stay calm,' Sabine said as she started using her hands to try and direct the current over his gills and get some oxygen flowing into his body.

'This is awful!' Jack exclaimed, floating next to Sabine without a clue what to do.

'How long has he been here?' Sabine looked to Ava.

'I didn't realise what was happening,' Ava cried, ignoring Sabine's question. 'I was pecking at the parasites in his teeth when Henry started jerking his head around so much that I thought I was going to be sick,' Ava wiped her eyes with her fin. 'I fell out of his mouth and saw that Henry's tail was caught in the shark net. The more he panicked and tried to free himself, the more the net wrapped around him.'

Gibbons and Finn watched as Sabine put her hands to the ropes and felt how tightly they had been knotted together. They were rough and thick from the water. She pulled at the different sections but they would not loosen at all.

Jack suddenly perked up. 'You know what we could do? Round up more angel fish and, together, gnaw through the ropes,' he said.

Sabine stopped and looked at Jack. 'That's a clever idea! We could split into groups and take different sections of the rope.'

'Yes!' Ava said, the idea of being able to do something calming her down for a second. 'Let's go and find more angel fish.'

'Or just any fish,' Emily said. 'Anyone who can chew.'

'Go! Jack, Ava, go and find help.' Sabine moved back towards Henry's head to carry on comforting him. Ava and Jack swam off. Sabine turned to Henry, who seemed to be glaring at her.

'You could have stopped all of this a long time ago,' he said suddenly.

Sabine jerked back, stung.

'What do you mean?' she asked.

'You're Alex's daughter and you've done nothing. Where have you been?'

Finn came forward. 'Come on, Henry. You know it's more complicated than that.'

'Five years! Scalewave is over because of her,' Henry snapped. 'You're just like a Land Creature,' he said to Sabine.

'Henry!' Emily exclaimed. 'That's a terrible thing to say.'

'You can choose who you want to be,' he retorted and rolled his eyes away from them.

'It isn't true!' Sabine wailed. She turned away and tilted her head down. Her shoulders started to shake, bubbles of air escaping as she sobbed. Emily put her flippers around Sabine's neck to comfort her, resting the base of her shell on

Sabine's shoulder. She shook her head at Henry, who looked ready to start weeping as well.

Meanwhile, Jack was racing after Ava. Really, though, even when Jack is racing, he's not going very fast. His little body was so light and his tail did not help him move through the water. The fins on the side of his head looked like extended ears; they helped him with his steering and balancing but they didn't create any speed, so it wasn't long before he lost sight of Ava. He beat his dorsal fin as hard as he could and tried to follow her bubble trail instead, but he soon lost sight of that as well.

He called out after her, 'Wait for me!'

He'd been caught up in the excitement of having a plan, but now, as he slowed and his heart rate came back down, he looked around and realised he was alone. He spun on the spot and all he saw in every direction was the deep, empty ocean.

'Ava?' He called out.

Nothing came back to him. No sound. No movement. He looked back in the direction Ava had gone and struggled on. His tail felt like it was dragging him down, his back ached and he couldn't see very far in front of him. After only another metre, he paused again. The ocean stretched away above and below. Henry had been caught in the middle layer of the ocean between the seabed and surface and he and Ava had stayed swimming on the same level. Small particles hung suspended, floating in front of him in the brilliant blue-green water. Jack suddenly felt a creepy sensation and he shivered. He turned around and started heading back the way he had come. He saw the outline of the net up ahead and made his way there, knowing that, if he followed it, he'd be sure to get back to Henry and Sabine. He swam alongside the netting, thinking all the while that it couldn't be much further. The water was cool and fresh. He tried to suck in lots of oxygen, but the longer it was taking, the more his panic rose. He pulled his rucksack off his back and, taking off his waistcoat, pulled on a jumper. He took out a fin-full of plankton and gobbled some down. The creepy feeling grew. He felt like he was being watched. He looked behind him. No one. He looked below him. No one. He turned back and looked ahead again. No one.

Then he looked up ... and there was a stingray unlike any he'd ever seen – not one of the cownose stingrays or the Atlantic torpedo stingrays that had been in their cavern before, but a totally different breed. It had a yellow body with blue spots and matching blue stripes running down its long tail.

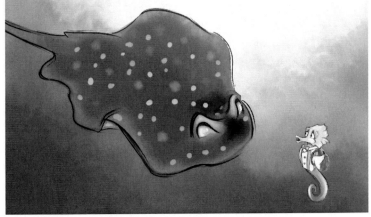

Jack knew immediately that this was a blue-spotted ribbontail stingray, a very dangerous ray with poisonous spines at the end of its tail. Even worse, this one had a mean face with yellow eyes protruding up and out of its flat body ... and these eyes were fixed firmly upon Jack.

'Stingray!' Jack yelled. 'STINGRAY!'

Silence. The stingray glided down towards him until it was level with Jack. They floated, facing each other. Jack was completely isolated, on his own, watching the predator square up to him.

'Stingray ...' he called out again, pitifully now. The word drifted away, lost in the ocean, and he knew he was very, very alone.

Chapter Five

An Octopus with Seven Tentacles

The blue-spotted stingray's eyes bored into the soul of his dinner. You could almost see drool escaping its mouth, washing away into the ocean as he prepared to eat Jack. It moved a fin-length forward. Jack hopped half a fin-length backward. It came another full fin-length forward. The stingray raised itself up so that its mouth, on the underside of its body, was above Jack – and then it charged. It opened his mouth wide and came down on top of the little seahorse. Jack tried to spin and duck out of the way, but the sucking force from the stingray's mouth drew him inside. It clamped down upon him, Jack's back inside the stingray's mouth, his head and tail hanging out. Jack wept and cried out.

'Sabine …' It was a weak and tear-filled sound that could barely be heard in the enormous body of ocean.

Then, suddenly, a young but steely voice came from above. 'Let him go, Kinslee!'

Jack couldn't see who it belonged to, hanging as he was out of Kinslee's mouth. Kinslee looked up and there, floating down towards them like a balloon that had just had its air let out, was Toyah.

Toyah, half the size of Kinslee but holding herself confidently, came to a stop in front of him and bravely faced him head on.

'Kinslee, let him go,' Toyah said again.

'Look at the baby cownose. Aren't you cute?' Kinslee sneered at her through his mouthful of seahorse. He continued sucking and Jack's tail slipped inside his mouth, so that now only his head was sticking out.

'It hurts!' Jack wailed. 'Let me go, *please* let me go.'

'The whole of the Scalewave team will be after you if you don't,' Toyah threatened.

'Oh, and they are sooooo scary,' Kinslee mumbled.

'Sabine is minutes away,' Toyah shot back.

Kinslee laughed. 'The fabled Sabine. The bedtime heroine that never was.' Kinslee had the upper fin but his open-mouthed arrogant talk was all Jack needed to seize his moment. He pushed his head forward, the momentum pulling his body and tail out of the stingray's mouth, and he did a somersault downwards towards freedom.

'Shouldn't talk with your mouth full,' Toyah said laughing and, reacting quickly, she swam forward, placing herself between Kinslee and Jack. Kinslee's expression immediately became angry – he'd lost his dinner and all because of a small cownose stingray. Kinslee was quite the stingray snob and a teenage cownose was no match for him. The two spines at the end of his tail stood up on end, long and thin with jagged edges sticking out. Toyah mirrored him, whipping her own barb upwards in an arc. They turned their backs on each other, squaring off. The sword fight was on!

Jack watched in helpless horror as Kinslee approached Toyah and brought his barb down towards her. Toyah brought her barb up to meet his and they began duelling, their long spikes crashing and smashing up against each other. This isn't something stingrays normally do but Kinslee was determined to get his dinner back. Kinslee was advancing, he was bigger and stronger and Toyah's barb, which was much smaller than Kinslee's, was no match. He pushed her backwards into Jack as he cowered behind her. Yet Toyah kept going, her barb flashing through the water and meeting Kinslee's. She twisted and turned, whipping herself back and forth, bravely protecting Jack. Jack stuck close to Toyah, using her body as a shield, and looked

frantically around for a way to help her ... when a clicking noise reached them and through the water came Marvin and Garvin, our two favourite Hawaiian spinner dolphins. In one easy swoop, Marvin knocked Kinslee up and away from Toyah with his nose. Garvin swam up to Jack, who latched onto his dorsal fin. Marvin doubled back and swam up to Toyah. The young stingray grabbed onto Marvin, and the dolphins swam Jack and Toyah away, leaving Kinslee still spinning in the water, hardly knowing what had hit him.

Emily was still trying to comfort both Sabine and Henry when, out of the blue, came Jack hitching a lift on Garvin, followed by Toyah clinging to Marvin.

'Sabine!' Jack let go of Garvin and flew through the water into her hands.

'Jack?' Sabine caught him and they looked closely at each other.

'Sabine? Have you been crying?' Jack asked.

Sabine nodded and asked him back, 'Have you?'

Jack nodded as well. 'I just took a holiday in a stingray's mouth.'

'It was Kinslee,' Garvin said, turning to Gibbons.

'Are you sure?' Gibbons said, shocked.

'Definitely,' Toyah said, letting go of Marvin.

'Are you ok?' Sabine checked Jack over and then looked to Gibbons questioningly.

'We need to check on Eli,' Finn said.

'Who's Kinslee?' Sabine asked.

'He is the stingray that The Kilk used to trap your parents,' Finn said.

Sabine, Jack and Emily's mouths all dropped open.

'Tanner was relaying a message when Kinslee intercepted him and changed the message, which led them into a trap.'

'I need to meet this Eli,' Sabine said firmly.

'Yes, we need to go. Follow me,' Gibbons said.

Sabine turned to Henry and looked directly into his one eye that was stuck looking on their side of the ocean. 'We will be back. I promise you,' she said.

And off the group went to find Eli, the octopus with seven tentacles.

*

The water was murkier here and it was hard to see. Sabine tuned into the freckle-like pores that were scattered on her cheeks and, soon enough, felt the vibration of a small structure about 30 fin lengths up ahead, just slightly off their course. She pushed her right hand through the water, keeping her left hand down by her waist, swinging her tail from side to side to propel forward and change direction. In the same way that a shark uses its pectoral fins for steering and balance. Sabine led the group as the vibrations coming back to her were getting stronger and stronger. The shadowy outline of an underwater sandcastle loomed through the misty water. A central dome structure with seven tunnels leading off from it stretched out in every direction. Shells decorated the tops of the tunnels like the slates on the roof of a house, and oysters lay in the sand, circling the outside like a moat that surrounds a castle. Two oval-shaped windows were set in the front of the dome above a rectangular hole in the middle, where a walkway had been moulded out of the sand to look like a drawbridge. On either side of the bridge, guarding the entrance, were two chocolate chip starfish. Their bodies were a light cookie-dough colour and they had rows of dark brown blob-like horns on top, just like chocolate chips! The starfish were clinging onto the wall of the castle, their bottom halves embedded in the sand and their top halves bending upwards, pressed into the base of the castle. The group approached cautiously and paused at the apparent entrance.

'Knock knock,' Gibbons called out. Marvin and Garvin added the clicking sounds from their tongues to attract attention.

A voice came from inside. 'Who is it?'

They all exchanged frightened glances except for Finn, who looked annoyed.

'Oh, so he's fine then,' Finn said.

'Finn?' the same voice called out.

'Eli, please could we have a word?'

'You need to leave!' the voice raged back.

The two chocolate chip starfish guards suddenly rose up, their chocolate chip-shaped horns protruding outwards aggressively. Everyone in the group apart from Finn backed

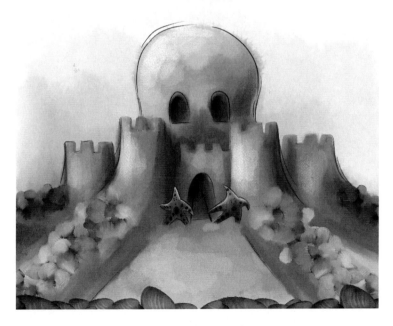

away. Emily looked to Jack, who seemed distracted and was staring in the opposite direction.

'Eli, we *really* need to talk to you,' Finn continued, coming to rest his long snake-like body on the sand and using his wavy fins on the top and bottom of his body to slither forward.

'You *really* need to leave!' it yelled again.

'Why weren't you at the meeting today?' Gibbons asked, coming up behind Finn. 'You know how important it was.'

Silence from inside. The group looked at each other, not sure what to do. They huddled together and began whispering.

Jack, however, hopped a few fin lengths away from them. He couldn't be sure, but it seemed as if the seaweed was moving – slowly and softly shifting position. He hadn't noticed at first, it was so gentle that it could have been the water making it ripple. Jack looked away for a few seconds. He moved his eyes around independently of each other, looking backwards and forwards at the same time – another one of his amazing skills. Then, when he looked back, it definitely appeared to have moved two fin lengths to the left. He turned back to Emily and, ducking down close to her ear, whispered, 'I think the seaweed just moved.'

'What?' Emily twisted her neck towards him and gave him a strange look, and then turned to follow the direction of his gaze towards the cluster of seaweed.

'That's what it does, Jack. It sways with the current,' she said.

'No, Emily, the seaweed MOVED. Like it moved its position.'

Jack and Emily huddled together, staring at the clump of seaweed.

'It was over there,' Jack nodded to the space where the seaweed had been, 'and *now* it's over there.' He pointed to where the seaweed had moved to. 'It's moved a few fin lengths towards us.'

Emily focused intently on the seaweed but nothing moved. She turned her head away and flicked it back quickly, and there ... The seaweed was moving sneakily towards them, but it stopped suddenly when she looked back at it. Emily curled her torn flipper around Jack protectively and backed away from it, pulling him along with her.

'We should tell Sabi,' she said.

Jack peered over the top of Emily's fin. This time, he was sure he saw eyes disappearing into the vegetation.

'Did you see that?' he hissed.

'I did!' Emily said.

Marvin glanced over, 'Are you ok, J-Em?' Emily turned to him and gestured to Sabine at the same time.

'The seaweed is moving,' Emily said.

'And it has EYES,' Jack added. Sabine turned and the four of them stared hard at the seaweed. Gibbons overheard and turned to look as well. Then his face dropped.

'Oh no,' Gibbons said. 'Oh no.'

At the same time, they heard Finn call out to Eli, 'Sabine is here ...'

They turned back to the sandcastle in time to see two large eyes appearing abruptly at the oval-shaped windows.

'Don't say another word,' the voice hollered, and, before another word could actually be said, the sand dome roof in the centre started to split – cracks splintered through as sand particles rolled off and dispersed into the water. Suddenly, the whole roof blew upwards as the head of a common octopus broke through and rose up and out of the sandcastle, a tentacle pulling out from each of the seven tunnels, following the head. Like a phoenix rising from the ashes, the octopus rose up from the sandcastle and floated above them. His seven good tentacles, long and a faded orange colour, waved softly up and down in the water. Where his eighth tentacle should have been, there was nothing but a stump – a nubbin, shrivelled in on

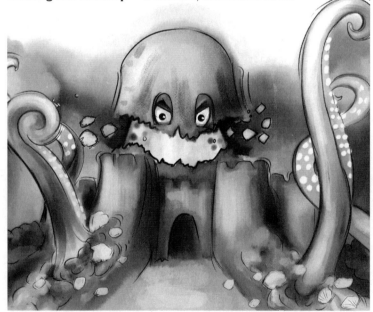

itself. The group looked up at him as if gazing upon a ghostly vision.

One tentacle reached up to his mouth and pressed against it as he whispered, 'Ssshhh . . .'

The group looked up at him and then to each other in confusion. Another tentacle lifted up and pointed to the seaweed.

'Weedy scorpionfish,' Finn said. 'Ugh!'

Jack looked again and then suddenly he saw it, the way you see a magic-eye picture change when you look at it slightly cross-eyed and another picture appears. Out of the seaweed, bodies emerged and branches turned into elaborate fins – they were actually weedy scorpionfish. An unusual looking fish in an incredible variety of shapes, colours and patterns that look a lot like seaweed. These ones were an array of light yellow, brown and green colours – a wonderful camouflaged disguise, perfect for sneaking up and eavesdropping!

'SPIES!' Eli hollered. 'They are spies for The Kilk. That's why I didn't make it today. I knew they were waiting outside to follow me.'

'Ohhh . . .' Finn said, looking panicked.

'And then you end up bringing Sabine to me,' Eli continued.

Gibbons swam over to the weedy scorpionfish and looked them directly in the eyes. The weedy scorpionfish quickly backed away, scared at being found out.

Marvin and Garvin made a suggestion. 'They've seen Sabine,' Marvin said. 'They should be held captive.'

'Stick them in Eli's castle,' Garvin said, 'and have the starfish guard them.'

'Good idea,' Eli agreed, and the two dolphins picked up the various weedy scorpionfish with their mouths, snapping at them quickly as they tried to scurry away and dropping them inside the centre of the sandcastle. Eli snapped two of his tentacles together and out of the sand appeared a Japanese white-spotted pufferfish. It quickly began building up the sandcastle again around the weedy scorpionfish, repairing all the damage Eli had done when he burst out of it.

'Thank you, Stefan,' Eli nodded to the little fish who was still raking through the particles in the sand, perfecting his creation.

Jack and Emily exchanged impressed glances.

'That was lucky,' Finn said, relieved not to have given the game away.

'Why are they watching you?' Gibbons asked. 'How did they know we were planning something?'

'I've no idea,' Finn said.

Eli turned to Sabine and said, 'Sabine, it's wonderful to see you again.'

'Um, you too?' Sabine said, completely unable to remember having ever seen this octopus before or, indeed, any octopus with only seven tentacles.

'You don't remember me, do you?' Eli asked.

'No I don't,' Sabine answered. 'Tell me about my father,' she said, wanting to get to the point. 'We saw Henry. He is in a terrible state and we want to save him.'

'Your father was a sharkmaid, Sabine. A Protector of the Seas, just like you are.'

'My mother too?' Sabine's eyes had gone wide and she stared into Eli's black ones where they sat at the top of his sack-shaped body.

Eli nodded, 'And without them, you are the only one left, which makes you The Last Guardian of the Ocean.'

Sabine looked seashell-shocked. 'What happened to them?' she asked.

'Your parents received a message that Land Creatures were killing blacktip reef sharks. They were fishing them out of the sea, cutting off their fins and throwing their bodies back into the ocean where they were left to die slowly,' Eli said.

Sabine stared at Eli, horrified.

'What on earth for?'

'They make soup out of them.'

'Yuck,' Jack said.

'Land Creatures kill 70 million sharks a year just for this shark-fin soup,' Eli said.

'Tanner was racing to your parents with the message. The Kilk captured Tanner and swapped him with Kinslee. Kinslee changed the co-ordinates of the location and led your parents into a trap where The Kilk set his sea spiders on them,' Eli gently explained.

'Sea spiders!' Jack turned his face towards Emily, who once again wrapped a flipper around Jack. 'What are they?'

'Pretty much what they sound like. Balls that look like urchins but with eight legs that wrap around their target. They inject their poison and it kills the victim,' Finn answered.

'You weren't supposed to be with them, but you had followed in secret. A sea spider saw you and attacked,' Eli continued.

'Alex, your father, grabbed it just as it was about to sink its teeth into you,' Gibbons said.

'Instead, it only grazed you with two of its teeth, but it was enough that you passed out.' Eli pointed to Sabine's dorsal fin, where two small notches were visible. Sabine reached around and felt them in shock.

'I thought these tears were a birthmark,' she whispered.

'Madison found you floating half a mile away, still unconscious. She took you to a lumpsucker fish who sucked out the poison, but when you woke you were so disorientated and confused. Madison suggested we take you to the Caribbean Sea while you recovered. But your memory never came back and then you disappeared,' Eli finished.

'There were reports of sightings of you,' Finn said, 'but we never quite knew what do to.'

'What happened to my parents?' Sabine asked.

'The sea spiders attacked them. Your father dropped his triton and it fell to the bottom of the ocean and got embedded in a rock,' Finn said.

'Then my parents are dead?' Sabine braced herself for the answer.

Finn looked over to Gibbons, who looked to Eli, who looked to Finn.

'Um ... maybe or, actually ... maybe not,' Finn stammered.

'We ... we're not actually sure,' Gibbons stuttered.

'We ... er, don't actually know ...' Eli spluttered.

'The poison reacted and instead of dying they ... grew legs,' Gibbons said.

'What kind of legs?' Sabine asked.

'Land Creature legs,' he answered.

'LAND CREATURE LEGS!' Sabine, Jack and Emily all exclaimed in unison.

'They couldn't swim with them, so two blacktip reef sharks ...' Gibbons said.

'... who still had their fins ...' Finn interrupted.

'... took your parents to the surface, but The Kilk came after them and attacked again. They fought back but then ... we lost track of them,' Gibbons continued.

'YOU LOST TRACK OF THEM!' the trio said, again in unison.

'They may have drowned when they became Land Creatures,' Eli finished.

'But you don't know?' Sabine snapped.

'No,' Eli said, looking devastated; Gibbons looked embarrassed.

'And we've been searching and arguing over you ever since,' Finn said.

*

The group hung around the sandcastle watching the weedy scorpionfish moan to be let out.

'So then, what's the plan?' Sabine asked.

'We have to get to the Guardian's Triton,' Eli said. 'Your father's triton.' He looked at Sabine pointedly and she frowned back at him.

'It's wedged into a piece of volcanic rock and it won't budge for anyone but its true owner,' Eli said.

'Who is its true owner?' Sabine asked.

'We're hoping it is you,' Finn said.

'But it might not be and it won't budge if it isn't?' Sabine looked back and forth between them all. Then she frowned again at Eli, feeling the weight of all their hope pressing upon her shoulders.

'Not if it doesn't belong to you,' Gibbons said.

'We could be putting ourselves in danger when we can't save the day anyway,' Jack said.

'You can go home,' Gibbons turned to Jack. 'You're not actually required.'

'He *is* required,' Sabine stated, and Jack didn't know whether to feel pleased or not.

'The triton is yours, Sabine. It will work for you,' Eli said, confident, ignoring the bickering. Sabine looked at him, trying to feel reassured. 'Once you get the triton and work with it, the powers it chooses will become instilled in you and they become yours. In effect, it is a training tool,' Eli continued.

'What does it look like?' Emily asked curiously.

'Like a pitchfork,' Finn said.

'That doesn't help,' Emily said. 'When was the last time you saw a pitchfork in the ocean?'

'All the time!' Finn said. 'Land Creatures are always throwing their mess into our world.'

'At least they don't know we're coming,' Gibbons said, ignoring him.

Toyah swam forward looking really scared.

'Toyah?' Emily asked, picking up on her fear.

'They may know Sabine is here.'

'How?' Everyone looked at her.

'I told Kinslee,' Toyah said, taking in a deep breath. 'I threatened him with Sabine when he was trying to eat Jack.'

'Oh, Toyah,' Finn said.

'I'm sorry!' Toyah wailed.

'Like it's not hard enough,' Gibbons snapped.

'I'm SO sorry,' Toyah said again.

'She was saving me,' Jack responded. 'She didn't have time to plan what to say.'

'Maybe Kinslee hasn't told The Kilk yet, or maybe he didn't believe me?' Toyah said hopefully.

'Let's get to the net,' Eli said. 'And plan our way over into *The Dark Wave*. Are you ready?' he asked, looking directly into Sabine's eyes.

Sabine shook her head and looked off into the distance. 'I need a moment.'

Eli nodded. 'Take a quick break,' he said.

Jack snorted, bubbles of air coming out of his mouth. As if a quick break was all they needed to prepare for this.

'I need to eat,' he said and started to sink.

'I need to breathe,' Emily said and started to rise.

Sabine watched as they headed off in opposite directions, Emily to the surface and Jack to the seabed. Sabine was glad to be alone for a moment. She floated in the middle of the huge ocean finning the water, looking around her and thinking about everything she had just heard. She felt a cold fear creep up inside her body and a tear escaped from her eye, immediately lost into the sea. She raised her tail in front of her and bent forward, wrapping herself up. Curled into a safe and cosy ball, she sank down into the depths to prepare herself mentally for what was coming next.

Chapter Six

A Leap of Fins

Gibbons, Finn and Eli were whispering in a huddle, half hidden amongst blades of seagrass. They were in the shallow waters at the tip of Morocco, not far from the border of *The Dark Wave*, where The Kilk's shark net was stretched out between the northern coast of Africa and the southern coast of Spain. Sunlight twinkled through the surface of the water and twirled upon the sandy seabed. Coral skeletons branched out like trees; anemones and urchins flowered into an amazing array of colours that shifted in the moving light. The three members of the Sea Council were deep in conversation and didn't notice Sabine approaching, along with Jack and Emily. Jack uncurled his tail from Sabine's hair and sailed towards a branch of yellow fan coral, his tail stretched out to its full length. He glided as easily as a monkey leaps from tree to tree, the dorsal fin on his back fluttering like a wing and propelling him forward. Jack came to land, wrapping his tail around the branch just as a pearly razorfish swam through the seagrass and towards him. Beams of rays picked out the red highlights on its fins that framed the upper and underside of its pink, scaly body. Jack leaned in and peeked over the fish, trying to hear their conversation.

'They're her friends,' Eli was saying to the other two. 'She needs them.'

'*We* need her focused, not worrying about those two,' Gibbons said.

'We don't want to risk upsetting her and losing her again,' Eli argued back. He glanced over and saw that the three of them were within earshot.

'What's going on?' Sabine asked as she swam over to where Jack was perched and confronted them.

Eli sighed and answered, 'Gibbons is concerned about Jack and Emily coming.'

'I thought we were a team,' Jack said.

'It's not about you,' Gibbons said. 'There's no I in team.'

'There is a me, though,' Jack muttered.

'Not really . . .' Gibbons shot back.

'There is if you rearrange the letters . . .' Emily said, backing up Jack.

'I thought you were gathering the masses, planning an uprising, putting together a movement . . .' Jack said, quoting what Sir Raynault had said in their cavern.

'Yes, and we're part of it,' Emily said. 'We will back Sabi up in any way we can.'

'We understand,' Eli said. 'Of course Sabine can choose who she wants to come with her.'

'Fine,' Gibbons said, sighing loudly.

Jack turned away and looked sad. Sabine moved over to him.

'Are you alright?' she asked him.

'He doesn't like me,' Jack said. 'Maybe I shouldn't talk so much?'

'They will think what they want to think, whatever you do,' Sabine told him.

'You are more honest and true to yourself than any sea creature I've ever met,' Emily said, swimming over to them.

'Embrace it. Own who you are,' Sabine said and held out her hand for Jack to swim into. He sat in her palm and rested his head on his chest, still feeling down. It reminded Sabine of when she first met Jack. She had heard him crying in the hands of a Chinese scuba diver, a Land Creature, who had been collecting seahorses to take home and put them into little plastic pouches, to then sell as living keyrings. These pouches have water with only enough nutrients to keep them alive for a few days and then they die. Sabine had come racing over and swam at the diver from behind. With her tail, she'd flicked loose the bag he was holding, cupped Jack in her palm and swam off with him, down into the deep ocean. Jack had sat there quite traumatized for some time.

Emily said to Jack, 'You're still only a young seahorse, don't be too hard on yourself. Wait till you are 67!'

'You're 67?' Jack exclaimed. 'So you're 64 years older than me?' he blinked as he checked his maths in his head.

'Yep,' Sabine said. 'And she's 55 years old than me! Emily is a wise old turtle.'

'I didn't know you had lived that long. I didn't know you could live that long,' Jack said to Emily in admiration.

'Well, we can when given the chance,' Emily said, 'but

there is so much stuff in the ocean now thanks to the Land Creatures, we're normally killed off before then.'

'Like my kind,' Jack said sadly.

Emily nodded. 'I went to take a bite out of a jellyfish a few years ago and started choking on this strange, clear and slimy material. Sabine had to put her hand in my mouth and pull it out.'

'I'm still not sure what is was,' Sabine said. 'But I am pretty sure it didn't come from the ocean.'

The three were quiet for a moment. Eli sensed a sadness and swam over to them, wanting to keep their spirits up.

'Let's get to the meeting place,' Eli said.

'Meeting place?' Sabine asked.

'Yes, we're meeting the rest of the troops over by the southern coral, directly in front of the shark net. Then we just have to figure out how everyone is going to get past it and over to the other side.'

The group swam along, led by Eli, with his seven brownish-red tentacles billowing out behind his head, stretching out wide and then squeezing back together and propelling his body forward. They rounded another bank of colourful coral, decorated with soft sponges and spiky-looking flowers. The coral is alive, made up of lots of coral polyps that secrete its skeleton onto the outside, protecting and supporting it. It was a brilliant hive of activity bathed in the sunshine glimmering down through the surface of the water.

'Oh good, they're here already,' Eli said, clearly relieved. Eli stretched out a tentacle, the circular suckers on the underside clearly visible, and gestured upwards. They followed the direction he was pointing in to where the coral fell away and the ocean opened out into a deeper, thicker blue. Marvin and Garvin were there, swimming back and forth, chattering away next to where a large group of 40 to 50 stingrays paraded in formation, barbs extended and eyes focused straight ahead. Watching them was Sir Raynault, floating next to a stern-looking, dark-coloured thornback ray. Both of them were wearing peaked army caps.

'Company ... halt!' the stern-looking ray yelled. The fever of rays stopped in unison and then he yelled, 'Company ... Form!' and the stingrays immediately started whizzing around. They swam over and under each other in a perfect choreographed dance until they were in three groups floating above each other, each in an arrow formation.

'Lieutenant Howes has been training the team for over a year now,' Gibbons informed them.

'They're taking this fight very personally,' Finn said.

Sabine blinked, unsure why it was so personal for them.

'Because of what he did to Scalewave. They loved your father and Tanner,' Eli explained, catching her expression.

'After all their hard work, they are keen to finally go over the top of the net and face The Kilk,' Gibbons said.

'Is Tanner coming?' Emily asked.

'No, he still won't leave his home. Lila is trying to help him deal with it but it's not easy after such a traumatic experience,' Finn told her.

'Kinslee has a lot to answer for, betraying all of the stingrays for a sea demon.' Toyah said.

'He was looking out for himself,' Finn told her.

'You said strands of cartilage are woven around the staff to strengthen it?' Sabine asked.

'Is the cartilage from sharks or rays?' Emily asked.

'Both,' Eli answered, 'because rays have evolved from sharks. The Kilk has been known to take cartilage from rays as well, but it's mostly sharks he is after.'

'Awful,' Jack said.

'There is a tooth at the top of his staff,' Finn said. 'The tooth of a megalodon.'

'No way! A megalodon?' Sabine's mouth dropped open.

'A what?' Jack said.

'A megalodon. It's a prehistoric shark. They were massive – bigger than the great white,' Sabine filled him in. 'They no longer exist.'

'The Kilk fought a battle with King Megalodon many years ago. He won and took one of its teeth.' Eli told them.

'The strands of cartilage at the top of the staff have been twisted into threads that wrap around into a cage. The tooth is protected inside,' Finn said. 'If we can pull that out, we can destroy the staff and disarm The Kilk.'

'So, it really is just a matter of distracting The Kilk, getting to his staff, and then pulling out the tooth,' Finn said.

'How are we supposed to get the tooth out of the staff?' Jack asked.

'One of us should be able to reach in and grab it,' Eli said.

'You could try sending Jack inside; he would fit,' Gibbons suggested.

'I told you he was required,' Sabine snipped at Gibbons and then looked over at Jack, whose eyes had gone very wide.

'We'll figure it out,' Sabine said to reassure him. 'Maybe my hand can squeeze inside.'

'How are we getting past the net and into *The Dark Wave*?' Emily asked.

'We either go over it, under it or through it,' Eli said.

'Surely we can just leap over it?' Sabine asked. 'I can clear the top of the net easily enough.'

'It does stick up a few fin lengths out of the water,' Eli responded, 'so you'll really have to leap high.'

'Easy,' Sabine laughed, having spent the last five years playing in the oceans around the Cayman Islands, leaping out of the water, spinning and splashing around.

'Ok,' Eli said. 'Sabine and the stingrays will go over it. Finn and I will go through it.'

'How will you do that?' Jack asked. 'You're way too big.'

'Octopuses don't have skeletons,' Eli explained, 'so I can squeeze through any gap. I just have to make sure my eyes can fit through!'

'Jack's small enough. He can come with us. What about Emily?' Finn said.

'I think Jack should stick with me,' Sabine said. 'He can anchor into my hair. Ems can attach to me by our bracelets. I don't want the three of us splitting up.'

'Ok. Marvin and Garvin will also go over it, so we're nearly ready,' Finn said.

'What about you?' Sabine looked to Gibbons.

'I'm not coming, I am too old. I will stay here,' and Gibbons looked over to where a shoal of striped eel fish were waiting for him. 'But I will be right behind you,' Gibbons said.

'How far behind us?' Emily asked.

'On the other side of the net,' Jack said flatly.

'Last words of caution before we go,' Eli said. 'Everyone, please be very careful and don't take any risks.'

'If the advice is to not take any risks, then let's not go!' Jack said and he turned around and started bouncing away.

'Don't be silly, Jack.' Sabine reached out her arm and, with one easy swoop, cupped him in her right hand and drew him back towards them.

Eli looked at Sabine seriously. 'If anything happens to any of us, you must keep going.'

'But what if . . .'

'. . . you keep going,' Eli cut her off. 'Now, are we ready?'

They moved closer to the net. The army of stingrays was lined up in their three groups, facing the large net, which stretched out dividing the Atlantic Ocean from the Mediterranean Sea. Sir Raynault was floating next to Lieutenant Howes.

'Company, prepare!' Howes yelled out and the stingrays all focused intently, looking straight ahead.

'Front-rays . . . ready . . . aim stingrays charged in unison. Like a flock of birds with instinctive precision, they raced towards the net and then rose up through the water and out into the air. Sabine and the group waited impatiently, watching for any signs that they had made it. Suddenly, swirling shapes could be made out dropping through the ocean on the other side of the net, surrounded by whirling bodies of bubbles.

'Blimey, they cleared it!' Jack yelled as, one by one, the outlines of the stingrays could be seen through the dispersing bubbles.

'Mid-rays, prepare!' Howes ordered and the next formation of stingrays came forward.

'Ready ... aim ... fire!' he bellowed, and the second set of stingrays raced towards the net and sailed over, splashing down on the other side.

'Hurray!' Sabine and Emily cheered, but they were quickly silenced by a look from Sir Raynault.

'Rear-rays, prepare!' Lieutenant Howes ordered once again and the final group of stingrays came forward.

'Ready ... aim ... fire!' he hollered one last time and the last line of rays shot forward in unison and leapt over the net, swooping down on the other side. Lieutenant Howes saluted Eli and Finn and followed the army over the net. Sir Raynault, though, had his eyes on Toyah.

'Toyah!' he called out to her. 'Enough sneaking around. You're not coming – now go home.'

'Dad!' she yelled back.

'No!' he responded. 'Home.'

Toyah nodded reluctantly and turned to the group. Jack came forward and floated in front of her.

'I didn't know he was your Dad,' Jack said.

'Right now, I wish he wasn't,' Toyah said.

'I wish you were coming,' Jack said.

'Me too. Take care of yourself, Jack.' They smiled at each other and Toyah backed away and then, satisfied, Sir Raynault turned and followed Lieutenant Howes over the net. Next, Marvin and Garvin raced forward and went spinning out of the ocean, over the net, landing gracefully on the other side.

'Excellent,' Eli said, pleased.

'Ok, Sabine, J-Em, you guys are up.' Finn said taking on the dolphin's pet name for the seahorse and turtle. Gibbons looked to Sabine. 'Once you're safely over, we'll swim through. See you on the other side!'

Sabine turned away from them and faced the net. Her heart started to beat faster as she prepared to make the leap. She clenched and unclenched her fists, took a deep breath in, and then, like an Olympic pole-vaulter, sprint-swam towards the net. To help her move faster through the water, Sabine kept both of her arms down by her waist to streamline her body. Emily drew her head into her shell, turned onto her side and tucked in towards Sabine. When she was only a few fin lengths away, Sabine lifted her head upwards to change direction, kicked her tail hard, and then, like a bullet, shot out of the water and up into the brisk, salty air. Jack clung to her, his tail clamped around her hair, firmly anchored. Emily spread her flippers wide like sails as they soared in a perfect arc and flew over the net. As they cleared it, Sabine angled her head and neck down to steer them and they dove head-first back into the ocean. Water splashed up over them in a frothy mix of bubbles and spray as they landed on the other side of the net, sinking down into *The Dark Wave.*

Chapter Seven

Barry, the Bowmouth Guitarfish

Sabine swam a few strokes, lifting her head and kicking her tail to come to a stop upright. She hovered, finning the water, as Jack and Emily untangled themselves. Then they all took in their new environment. It was dark and dank. The water felt heavier, slimier, leaving a stickiness on their fins. Specks of dirt hung in the water, making it murky and hard to see through. The rocks were bare – dull browns and greys – and all the vibrancy was gone. No plants or algae grew; no fish were in sight. The ocean felt drained of colour, as if a light switch had been dimmed. The trio saw Eli and Finn slipping through the squares in the net, Eli's large head crushing down to squeeze through one of the small gaps. Jack watched, mesmerised by how Eli moved; it was so graceful and elegant. The duo swam over to join them.

'Well done,' Eli said. 'All ok?'

Sabine nodded, still looking around. It was a stark contrast to the life on the other side. 'This is awful,' she said. 'It's so hard to breathe.'

'It's suffocating,' Jack said, shocked by the barren landscape.

'It's becoming a Dead Zone,' Eli said.

'What's a Dead Zone?' Jack asked.

'A place where plants cannot grow due to a lack of oxygen,' Finn answered.

'This is happening around the world because of the waste that gets put into the ocean by the Land Creatures. Too many chemicals and nutrients cause lots of algae blooms to grow on the surface. This stops oxygen reaching further down into the ocean. Without oxygen, the sea life and animals either die or have to leave the area,' Eli informed them.

'It affects the whole balance of the underwater world,' Finn said.

'But, here, it's The Kilk who is destroying this area by capturing and killing all the sharks trapped in the Mediterranean,' Eli said.

'Let's accompany the army of stingrays and get to the base,' Finn said.

'Where's the base?' Sabine asked.

'It's a little way off from the south coast of Malta,' Eli said. 'There's a shipwreck in the Mediterranean Sea that we'll pass on our way.' He looked over to where the army of rays was hovering in its groups. Nearby, Lieutenant Howes and Sir Raynault waited patiently.

'We'll swim there and regroup before the next push to the Guardian's Triton,' Finn said.

Eli nodded to Lieutenant Howes, who yelled, 'Company ... advance!' and the procession – made up of an army of stingrays and their commanders, two dolphins, an octopus, an eel, a turtle, a seahorse and a sharkmaid – swam through the Alboran Sea, heading eastwards towards the Mediterranean Sea.

The convoy was travelling in groups: Eli and Finn were in front with Sabine and her two friends behind them. The stingrays fanned out around, escorting them. Marvin and Garvin were everywhere. They seemed to enjoy shooting ahead, doubling back, and then disappearing off again.

'If it's the sharks that are being killed off here,' Jack asked, picking up the conversation they had been having earlier, 'then how is it affecting the oxygen and causing a Dead Zone?'

'Sharks are apex predators,' Eli said.

'Apex ... what?' Jack said.

'They are at the top of the food chain and control the balance of the food below them,' Finn answered for Eli.

'Without sharks, the fish below them grow in larger numbers and then they eat all the fish that are below them. When there are no little fish left that eat algae, then too much vegetation grows and that sucks up all the oxygen,' Eli explained.

Jack was silent, taking all this in. 'Wow,' he said finally, looking at Sabine, whose eyebrows were raised, also amazed.

'So it had the same effect that dumping waste into the ocean has,' Finn finished.

'Wow,' Jack said again and they continued on in silence.

It was a long journey to the base and Jack sat in Sabine's shoulder-length hair in his usual position, hitching a ride. He munched on the plankton he'd packed into his rucksack, forever the hungry seahorse.

'I'm getting low on snacks,' he told Sabine as they swam along.

'Why don't you open up your rucksack wide at the top and drag it along to catch some plankton?' she suggested.

'I thought of that,' Jack said, 'but I haven't seen any plankton at all.'

'I'm hungry too,' Emily acknowledged, and, for the first time ever, Jack reached into his bag with his nose and nudged some small molluscs towards Emily.

'Thank you,' Emily said, as she took a flipper-full of molluscs and gratefully munched them down.

Suddenly, Marvin and Garvin came swimming back to them, calling out, 'There's something up ahead!'

'What?' Eli yelled back, as he looked up and saw a shadow in the distance swimming slowly towards them. It was higher up, in a different level of the ocean body, and it was hard to make out its shape. It seemed to be a ray swimming in front of a shark. They sprint-swam over to a bare bank of coral and ducked down behind it, pressing themselves low into the rock. The army of stingrays instinctively formed around the group.

'It's ok!' Marvin called out from the top of the lifeless rock. 'It's not The Kilk – there's a shark up ahead.'

'What type of shark?' Sabine asked curiously.

'That's not a shark, it's a . . .' Garvin started to answer, as he squinted at the creature between a gap in the rock.

'Oh, actually, I think it's a ray . . .' Marvin said uncertainly.

'I don't think so,' Sabine said as she lifted her head and peeked over the edge of a ridge to look at the strangest creature she'd ever seen. 'What *is* that?'

Its brownish body was long and sleek like a shark. It had a dorsal fin and a large tail fin, but it also had a second dorsal fin halfway down its back. Its head was wide and flat – similar to the shape of a ray. It even had the same fins on the sides of its head that rays have on the sides of their bodies. It was decorated all over with white spots and it had a row of dark thorns that ran behind its head and down its body towards its dorsal fins. Sabine thought how useful they must be for protection against predators.

'It looks like a guitar,' Jack said, venturing out to rest on Sabine's shoulder.

'A guitar-fish,' Sabine said, laughing.

'It's a bowmouth guitarfish,' Emily said.

Jack and Sabine laughed.

'No, really!' Emily said. 'It's basically a shark ray and yet it's neither shark nor ray.'

'So cool!' Marvin said. 'We don't get those over in Hawaii.'

'It's a bit like me,' Sabine said, 'neither shark nor Land Creature.'

'The bowmouth guitarfish's white underbody is a really clever design,' Emily explained to them. 'Like with sharks, their white underside means it's hard for a predator to see them when looking up from below, because they blend in with the light from above. Then their darker top side makes it hard for prey to see them when looking down, because they blend in with the darkness below. Lots of sharks have a white underbelly for the same reason. Isn't that clever!' She stated.

'Wow,' Sabine said. 'It really is.'

'It's been ages since I saw a bowmouth guitarfish,' Emily said.

'Yes,' said Finn. 'They are endangered.'

'What does that mean?' Jack asked.

'It means there are so few of them left that they are in danger of totally disappearing – of no longer existing anywhere on the planet.' Finn told him.

'That's so sad,' Jack said.

'Shame it got stuck this side of the net,' Emily said.

'Many animals got stuck because they had no clue what was going to happen and the net went up suddenly overnight,' Eli said.

'Once your parents disappeared, they had no one to protect them,' Finn added.

The bowmouth guitarfish was meandering towards them. He seemed to have few cares in the world as he was going very slowly, which, given the fear and tension on this side of the net, was very odd. They slowly swam up from behind the rock and paused, watching the creature and waiting for him to notice them. Suddenly, his eyes flickered in their direction and he stopped as he took in the strange group. A look of fear passed across his face. Then, pretending he hadn't seen them, he slowly turned and started to swim away.

'Oh, wait. I think that's Barry,' Finn said, as the bowmouth guitarfish started to speed up and swim away. Marvin and Garvin chased after him with Finn following.

'Barry, wait!' Finn hollered through the ocean.

'Hey! We want to help,' Garvin said.

The bowmouth guitarfish could sense them behind him and he did another U-turn to face them. He looked very carefully at the two dolphins, Finn lagging behind, trying to catch up. Sabine came over but hung back, keeping her distance.

'What do you want?' Barry asked.

'We're staging an intervention with The Kilk,' Marvin answered.

'What?' Barry didn't look impressed. 'And how are you going to do that?'

Suddenly, Finn pushed forward and said, 'Barry? It's me!'

'Finn?' Barry said, looking very shocked.

'How are you two friends?' Garvin asked.

'There are lots of unlikely friendships in the sea,' Finn said. 'Look at Eli and myself.'

'So are you part of this 'intervention'?' Barry asked.

'I am,' Finn said proudly.

'We're going to get the Guardian's Triton,' Marvin said.

'I thought dolphins were supposed to be smart,' Barry replied.

'We are!' Marvin said, indignant.

'We're also brave,' Garvin said.

'Intelligent and brave – a combination that normally leads full circle to stupidity,' the bowmouth guitarfish said. 'Do you know how many of us have tried to lift the Guardian's Triton?' Barry asked. 'It won't budge for anyone but Alex and he's gone. There is no hope; it's futile.'

Sabine was now within earshot and she swam up,

annoyed, and said to him, 'You could thank them for trying instead of calling them names.'

The bowmouth guitarfish was taken aback.

'Who are you?' he asked, frowning deeply as he took in Sabine's unusual shape.

'I'm Sabine,' she answered and put her hands on her hips, waiting to be challenged, but the bowmouth guitarfish looked stunned instead.

'Of course, wow!' Barry seemed like he wasn't going to say anything else as he floated there staring at Sabine in awe. Then finally he collected himself. 'It's a pleasure to meet you,' he said. 'My name is Barry.'

'Oh,' Sabine said, surprised at this change in his manner.

'So is it you who's going to get the Guardian's Triton?' he asked, becoming very excited.

'I'm going to try . . .' Sabine trailed off.

'This is incredible, we must go back and tell the others.' Barry started to take off.

'Others?' Eli asked, as he and the rest of them came over.

'There's a group of us hiding in a sunken oil tanker off the southern coast of Malta,' Barry said, looking back.

'Oh! That's where we are headed for,' Eli said. 'We're going to use it as a base.'

'Great, I'll take you!' Barry said.

'Why are you out here then?' Finn asked. 'It's really dangerous.'

'It was my turn to look for food,' Barry answered.

'That's crazy! With your body full of cartilage, you are a prime target for The Kilk,' Finn told him.

'There's no food,' Barry said. 'I had no choice really, we need to take it in turns so that it's fair on all of us.'

'That's brave,' Sabine said.

'As long as we swim at the designated swim speed, we don't attract much attention,' Barry told her.

'How fast is that?' Emily asked.

'We're not allowed to cover more than 500 fin lengths in a day,' Barry answered.

'Oh, so that's why you were swimming so slowly,' Marvin said.

'Can we stop chit-chatting and keep moving, please?' Sir Raynault called out from where he was floating, some way off. Barry looked around, taking in the whole group.

'You're quite an interesting bunch, aren't you?' he observed.

'The balance of the ecosystem is everyone's problem,' Eli said.

'Indeed,' Barry agreed, and smiled at Sabine, who was really feeling the pressure of being the sea creature that everyone needed to save the day.

'Let's move it, please,' Sir Raynault called out and the whole company, with their new addition, took off – this time with Barry leading the way.

The ship stood upright, broken and bent out of shape, its base buried into the seabed. Split into two parts, it was resting silent and still. As they swam towards it, low beams of sunshine cast a spooky glow upon the wreck. The metal was rusted a brown and green, the salty water eating away at it and making patches of white and grey. Around the ship were purple sea urchins, floating listlessly. It was the only colour they had seen since entering *The Dark Wave*. Normally, the wreck would have been teeming with fish and covered in algae, but here too the ocean was deserted of life save for the sea urchins.

'We need to watch out for Land Creatures,' Barry said as he slowed on the approach. 'They dive a lot here.'

They swam up to it and floated above the ship, looking down. The stingrays spread out, checking the area.

'It wasn't actually sunk here,' Barry continued. 'It was dragged here by Land Creatures to try and create an artificial reef to help a bigger variety of fish develop.'

'Oh, so the Land Creatures are trying to help then?' Sabine asked.

'Some of them,' Eli answered for Barry.

One of the urchins floated in front of Jack. It was a small circular ball covered in dark-red spines. He went towards it and, as he reached out his head, Emily chipped in quickly … 'Don't touch them,' she said. 'I know it's tempting but you never know what might be poisonous.'

'Or you might accidentally kill it,' Sabine said. 'A lot of sea life dies when we touch it.'

But the urchin came to life in front of their eyes. It hung suspended in front of them, the boldness of its colours changing in the shadowy water. Jack pulled his head back and stared at it.

'Ooooh, it's so pretty,' he said, quite mesmerised. As he bobbed there, taking in the surprising beauty of the urchin in these cold, depressing waters, other urchins started popping up, rising to meet him.

'Hang on …' Eli said, coming over. 'I'm not sure …' but before he could finish what he was saying, the urchins uncurled themselves. One by one, in front of their eyes, legs appeared … one, two, three, four. Long, thin and angular, they were jointed at the middle like two thirds of a triangle. Jack started to bob away in surprise, amazed. But they weren't done, more legs came … Five, six, seven, eight … The round, ball-shaped body was now at the centre of each, with eight legs sticking out.

'Are these sea spiders?' Emily cried out, looking like her deepest, darkest nightmares had just materialised in front of her eyes. Jack swung backwards in terror. Sabine stared in horror.

'Ambush!' Sir Raynault yelled.

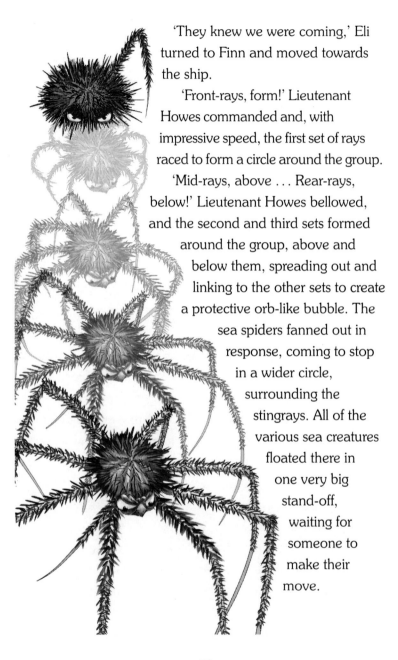

'They knew we were coming,' Eli turned to Finn and moved towards the ship.

'Front-rays, form!' Lieutenant Howes commanded and, with impressive speed, the first set of rays raced to form a circle around the group.

'Mid-rays, above ... Rear-rays, below!' Lieutenant Howes bellowed, and the second and third sets formed around the group, above and below them, spreading out and linking to the other sets to create a protective orb-like bubble. The sea spiders fanned out in response, coming to stop in a wider circle, surrounding the stingrays. All of the various sea creatures floated there in one very big stand-off, waiting for someone to make their move.

Chapter Eight

The Triton in the Rock

The biggest, blackest sea spider rose up through the dirty, murky water to look directly at Eli.

'How's your stubbin of a nubbin, Eli?' it jeered at him.

'Quite comfortable, Esra,' Eli said. 'There's less drag when I swim now.'

'What are you lot doing here?' a scary, and very hairy, female sea spider said, coming forward.

'We've missed you, Deniella,' Finn said, mocking her.

'Getting ready to lose another tentacle?' Esra smirked.

'Turn around and go home,' Deniella said.

'No,' Eli said. 'You can't scare us.'

'Are you sure about that?' Esra asked, and turned to look behind him.

They followed his gaze and through the midst of sea spiders rose a large blue-spotted stingray. A few thin beams of sunlight pierced down through the ocean and picked out the blue dots covering his yellow back, causing them to glow. His yellow eyes stuck upwards, giving him a very wide view of everyone.

'Kinslee. The turncoat,' Eli stated.

'Keep well back,' Finn whispered to the group. 'The spines on his tail are extremely poisonous.'

'J-Em, stay close to Sabine,' Marvin nodded towards her.

Jack didn't need to be told twice. He leapt into Sabine's hair and, for the first time ever, camouflaged himself in it, taking on the dark brown colour of her strands. Emily peered at where she had last seen Jack and struggled to make him out. He had tangled himself into Sabine's hair and blended in. Emily was impressed and floated closer to Sabine so that she was hovering just to the side of her.

'How could you?' Eli said to Kinslee.

'How could I choose the side that was the biggest and the best? Haven't you heard of the survival of the fittest?' Kinslee sneered at him.

'At the cost of your self-respect?' Eli asked.

'That's a low price to pay for food and power,' Kinslee told them.

'Only if you care for no one else,' Finn said.

'Where's The Kilk?' Eli asked.

'Behind you,' Esra said.

Eli went stock-still. Gripped by fear, he slowly looked behind him ... but no one was there, save for the trio, the dolphins, Barry and the circle of stingrays. He turned back to Kinslee and glared at him. Kinslee grinned and then started to back away.

'Come back here,' Eli demanded, but Kinslee turned his back on him.

It was clearly the signal to attack. The sea spiders came forwards, Esra heading straight for Eli and Deniella heading for Finn.

The army of stingrays was poised, ready to respond, but they didn't move. Any second now ... but no ... they still didn't move. When the sea spiders were just a few fin lengths away and starting to look a bit uncertain at the expressionless, motionless rays, Lieutenant Howes bellowed 'Activate plan!' and another orchestrated dance came to life.

The front-rays swarmed together in unison, each racing towards the sea spider nearest to them. The mid-rays came closer to Sabine, Jack and Emily, and formed a tight circle around them. The rear-rays, led by Sir Raynault, went after Kinslee.

'You're mine, Kinslee!' Sir Raynault called out to him as Kinslee raced away and out of sight.

As the front-rays got closer to each approaching sea spider, they ducked down below them and swam underneath to rise up on the other side, behind each one. The sea spiders turned around in confusion and the rays charged again. This time, the sea spiders stuck all of their legs downwards, ready for the rays to duck, but the stingrays instead shot upwards and over them. They rose up and dove down, ducking and diving, avoiding the sea spiders' legs in an impressive display.

Finn dodged Deniella, his thin body slithering away like a serpent. Esra came straight at Eli and aimed at a tentacle. He laughed and said, 'Shall I go for the whole set?' Esra's voice was cruel and harsh.

Eli pulled all his tentacles down, squeezed them together and shot upwards, out of Esra's way. Deniella came up below him and extended a leg, aiming for Eli. Finn shot towards Deniella and wrapped his long, thin body around her, crushing her legs together.

Esra came up again, reaching out for Eli. Eli slid out a tentacle towards Esra's outstretched legs and grabbed one, tugging hard. It came away from Esra's body.

'And now we're even,' Eli said, as he let go of the leg and it sank down into the ocean.

'Seven tentacles to seven legs!' Finn cheered, still holding onto Deniella, who kept squirming as she tried to break loose.

Sabine looked to where Kinslee and Sir Raynault had gone, but she couldn't see either of them. The dolphins hung back with the trio and Barry, watching the scene unfold. The rays spun and whirled, twisted and twirled – yet it was no easy battle. The sea spiders have eight legs to fight with, which are positioned all around their circular bodies. The stingrays have one barb at the back of their bodies, so they have to move carefully – but a year's worth of training and practice were paying off and the stingrays were gaining the upper fin. They extended their barbs, aiming for the centre of the sea spiders, and swam underneath them again, taking shots from below. The barbs pierced into their middles and the sea spiders cried out in pain.

Suddenly, Sir Raynault came racing back through the water, fear and dread all over his face. He was followed by the team of rear-rays. Eli and Finn stared at them in confusion. Then, behind Sir Raynault, a shape appeared. It sped through the water like a torpedo and smashed straight into the fighting, aiming for the rays.

Lieutenant Howes stared in shock. Eli paused in horror. Finn relaxed his grip on Deniella, nearly letting her break free.

Jaws wide and gaping, the killer whale attacked, its mouth crashing shut on some of the stingrays – one of its favourite foods. The surprise strike gave the sea spiders an advantage. A few of the smaller Atlantic torpedo stingrays were caught, the sea spiders wrapping their legs around them and piercing them with their teeth. The poison acted immediately and, when the sea spiders let go, the rays sank down to the sandy seabed where they lay unmoving.

Marvin and Garvin pulled off their sunglasses.

'The glasses are off!' Garvin called out, as he and Marvin charged at the killer whale, spinning around it and taking bites out of its sides. The killer whale turned to bite back at them.

Eli was spinning on the spot, his tentacles stretched out and smacking into as many sea spiders as possible. He turned to Sabine as the mid-rays broke away to help the others.

'Go!' Eli yelled.

'No!' Sabine yelled back, coming forwards.

'Sabine, get the triton,' Eli yelled again, as he was swamped by more sea spiders.

Still Sabine hovered, torn.

'It's the only way to help us,' Finn called out.

'This way,' Barry said, and turned towards the shipwreck.

Emily looked to Sabine. Her eyes were misty with fear, but then it seemed to part like the clouds and was replaced with glistening determination. Sabine reached out her wrist and, in one swift and practised move, Emily stretched out her flipper and clipped her bracelet to Sabine's. Jack shook off his camouflage so they could see him and the trio went after Barry.

The ship's railings were broken and twisted, bent into different angles, moss lining them like a fur coat. Instead of the normal greenish tint, the moss was blackened and thinning from the lack of oxygen. Barry led the way over crumpled metal and steel towards the captain's cabin at the top of the ship. A large black hole where a door should have been led inside. It was a very small entrance and Barry had to squeeze through. Sabine followed and ducked through the doorway, looking up as she entered, unsure why they were entering the ship where they would be trapped and unable to escape. Barry carried on down through the captain's cabin into the belly of the wreck, past the internal staircase, brown and rusty with age and erosion, and right down to the base of the ship, known as the hold. The three looked around cautiously as they followed him into what looked like a large open room. It was even darker down here, but a light was glowing from a species of fish that was dotted around the room: barreleye fish. These deep-water fish were here inside the shipwreck casting illumination onto the other fish that were filling the hold. Fish and sea creatures were everywhere: purple tang fish, porkfish, trumpetfish, hermit crabs, starfish and jellyfish. They were all hiding out together in the base of the sunken boat.

'Look who I've found!' Barry said.

The fish, wide-eyed, gathered around.

'Sabine?' A black goby fish came closer. 'How?'

'It's a long story,' Sabine said, swimming around in a full circle to take it all in.

'I can't believe you are all hiding in here,' Emily said.

'It is getting a bit crowded,' the black goby fish said.

'I want to help you all,' Sabine said and turned to Barry. 'But I need to get out of here. I need to help Eli.'

'Over there . . .' Barry nosed his way to the bottom of the metal ship and, using his fin, flicked a catch on a circular door. The black goby fish came over to help and, together with a hermit crab, they pulled open the door to reveal a long tunnel leading down into the earth underneath the sea.

'Oh wow,' Jack breathed out, as Sabine swam over and looked inside.

'You can travel safely out of here through this tunnel. We've spent the last five years building up a maze of underwater tunnels.'

'Incredible,' Sabine said.

'I'll lead the way so you don't get lost,' Barry said. 'There's a route that takes you into the heart of the Mediterranean Sea and will get you close to the location of the triton.'

A cheer went up around the room but Sabine looked stressed and Barry, catching her look, dove straight into the tunnel. Sabine followed, with Jack still hitching a ride in her hair and Emily following behind instead of being clipped to Sabine, as they travelled at a slower pace through the network of tunnels.

It was cool and dark and they could barely see. Barry had clearly been doing this a long time and knew his way around. The minutes ticked by and Sabine kept kicking her tail, surging forwards in frustration.

Eventually, a distant
spark of light could
be seen up ahead,
and shortly they
reached the opening
of the tunnel. Barry
peered out of the
entrance and looked
around.

'All clear,' he said
and swam out. The
trio followed him.

It was another bleak and empty place. The tunnel exit was carved into a mound of earth sticking out of the seabed. A few fins lengths ahead, the seabed took a sudden dip and disappeared into murky depths.

'Keep swimming, heading south,' Barry said. 'It is not far from here. Head straight there and stick to the swim limit.'

They took one last look at each other, before Sabine thanked him and swam off and over the edge, where the seabed dropped away. It was as if she had flown off a cliff. The mass of dark ocean lay beneath them – a mystifying black hole. As they descended further and further into the depths of the Mediterranean Sea, the water became murkier and murkier. Flecks of sea matter floated listlessly, carried along by dark and unseen currents. Sabine paused and glanced back up, unable to make out the surface of the water anymore. She took a long breath in and slowly let it out to steady her nerves. Then she firmly kicked her tail and plunged onwards. It was colder here, the further they went down, without any warmth from the sun. The chill seemed to seep right in to the depths of their beings. Sabine shivered. Jack pulled his jumper out of his rucksack and pulled it over his waistcoat. Emily ducked her head into her shell and peered out nervously.

They continued onwards, swimming further and further down into the depths, until finally the seabed came into sight. Dark sea corals decorated the ocean bed here. Better able to live without oxygen and light, they had survived where the rest of the ocean had suffered.

'I think I can feel it,' Sabine said suddenly, pausing to take in the pulses of electricity that she was picking up on. She stopped and looked around, then altered their direction slightly to keep heading south and carried on. She was starting to feel excited for the first time – new waves of adrenaline pushing her forwards.

Jagged and blackened pieces of rock from volcanic eruptions long ago rose from the seabed like dark monsters. In the centre of the cluster, a sliver of dark red stuck up high, barely visible in the gloomy water.

Sabine swam a little closer, trying to make it out through the cloudy water, and then paused to take in the Guardian's Triton. The length of it was a dark red, made from pieces of red soft coral. Its end was woven with strands of bladderwrack wrapped around and around to form a thick and spongy handle. The top branched out into fire coral and split into three prongs. Tiny pieces of coral were coming off each section and waving softly in the water. Each prong was wedged firmly into the black rock, so only the bottom half and the base of the head where it connected to the staff were visible.

Sabine swayed her tail gently and approached the triton slowly. Jack and Emily looked around, searching for any signs of movement or sudden appearances of beautiful urchins that might actually be sea spiders, but all was still and quiet. Sabine swam to just half a fin length away.

She reached out her hand and held it above the handle of the triton, then jerked her arm back suddenly.

'What if they are wrong?' she said, turning to her two friends. 'What if I can't help and we are left out here exposed?'

'It's a bit late now,' Jack said gently.

'Go for it, Sabine. It's the only way to find out,' Emily said.

'Then you will know you have done all you can ...' Jack added.

'... and no one can ask for more than that,' Emily finished for him.

Sabine nodded, looking at them both but barely seeing them, lost in a world of imagined possibilities of what might be about to happen. She turned back to the triton as if in a trance and reached out her hand. She curled her fingers around the handle, feeling both the smoothness of the bladderwrack and the buzzing electricity of the triton's power. She took a deep breath in, pulled her arm back ... and in one fluid movement drew the triton out of the rock.

Chapter Nine

The Kilk

Sabine held the triton in her right hand and stared up at it. Jack and Emily floated next to her, wide-eyed and enthralled. It was a brilliant red and patchy in places from the natural colour of the coral. The dark-brown bladder-wrack handle gave way to a rough and knobbly length of stick. The top broke out into three spears – the ends of which were sharp and piercing. Sabine held it by the soft seaweed handle and ran her thumb over a bump just above the fraying edges, feeling the life pulsating from within. All three gazed at it, taking it in.

'It's yours . . .' Jack breathed out in wonder.

'You're The Guardian of the Ocean,' Emily said.

Sabine could not stop the massive grin that spread across her face. She brought her hand down, pulling the triton towards her to examine it up close. The three-pronged head was more intricate than it had first appeared. Tiny twig-like strands of fiery coral reached out from each spike and wove together, interlacing. The spears that had been embedded in the rock were dull and discoloured; specks broke off and floated away into the cloudy water. She looked to her friends and wrapped her arms around them into a big hug, a huge grin on her face. Emily did a backflip and Sabine twirled on the spot. Jack bopped, shaking his waist from side to side until he got too hot and had to take off his jumper and put his waistcoat back on!

'Ok,' Sabine said. 'Let's get back to the tunnel . . .'

As she turned to swim away, she looked down and noticed a line of bubbles trailing out in front of her. She looked to see what its source was, but there was nothing there. Jack and Emily looked down curiously and then up at each other. They hovered there in silence, glancing around, and then . . . a whooshing noise sounded and a large blast of bubbles streamed through the ocean and around them like a mist, and slowly the hazy outline of a creature became clear.

His head was horse-like, thin and narrow. It arched down to his neck and then widened out into a thick body that then thinned out again into small frog legs with fins hanging off that seemed to merge into the sea, so it was hard to see where his body ended. He seemed to be made of the water itself, held together by a thin casing of water-like skin; he blended into the sea so that there was no clear division between him and the swirling bubbles of ocean he swam through. He had frog-like arms and in place of fins, Sabine could see webbing stretching out from each arm down to the sides of his waist like the wings on a bat. There was more webbing between each of his fingers and he had long nails like the talons of the birds of prey she has seen swooping down to the ocean to hunt fish. He held his staff in his left hand. It was long and thin with strands of the flexible, white cartilage woven together, twisting round and round up the length of the cane. At the top, four strands of cartilage curled

around to create a sphere, within which the large tooth of King Megalodon sat. It was ginormous. If Sabine had rested it in her palms, it would have covered both of her hands.

The Kilk turned and swam away, whizzing back through the water to disappear into it. Sabine went after him, but he was gone. Emily clutched Jack in her flippers, hiding behind the rock where the triton had spent five years waiting to be claimed. Sabine heard the rushing sound of water behind her and turned to see him rising up with his arms out wide, the wing-like fins stretched out like a web. He threw his staff from his left hand to his right and, without pausing, raised it up high and then brought it down to strike Sabine. She raised her triton to defend herself and the two weapons smashed against each other. They pulled them back and crashed them together again, struggling back and forth. The water eddied and churned. The sand swirled up off the seabed, tiny pieces of crystal and seashells whipping into a whirlpool. They started to rise as they fought higher and higher through the water. Jack and Emily followed, starting to come forward, ready to leap in and help where they could, but then Jack suddenly gasped. Rising up in front of them, three orange urchins had appeared through the water.

'No!' Jack cried out and he and Emily started to back away, knowing exactly what was about to happen. Sure enough, the urchins uncurled their eight legs and spread themselves out wide, expanding into sea spiders. They swam towards the cowering Jack and Emily from either side and spread their legs out, over and around them to meet each other, imprisoning the seahorse and turtle inside a makeshift cage made out of their 24 legs. Inside, Jack and Emily huddled together, looking at the sea spiders' mouths, which were full of poisonous teeth that were barely a tenth of a fin length away.

Sabine looked down at her friends in a panic and, with a powerful burst, wielded her triton at The Kilk. He deflected her aim and returned with his own hit. They continued to rise up and up through the water, circling each other, trading blows. The sea spiders, holding their cage of prisoners, rose with them, following the battle.

Emily peered out between the sea spiders' dark orange legs and stared through the foggy water at a shadowy shape some way off.

'Jack!' Emily said to him and Jack turned and looked out at the small shape, which was growing steadily bigger and bigger. They stared hard. Coming into focus was a round shape, long legs fanning out and then disappearing behind the body. 'Eli!' Emily called through the legs surrounding her. 'Eli, over here!'

Eli steamed towards them. He stretched out his tentacles all around his body and spun towards the cage of sea spiders' legs and smacked into it with six good tentacles. The cage of spiders broke open and they yowled with pain and rubbed their legs together attempting to soothe them. Jack and Emily swam out – Jack trying to propel his little body along as fast as he could. Emily reached back and pulled him along with he flippers. Sabine and The Kilk each caught the action out of the corner of their eye and turned towards them. Sabine quickly swam over to her friends.

Jack and Emily leapt to Sabine. Emily wrapped her flippers around Sabine's left forearm, her shell facing outwards and acting like a shield. Jack jumped onto Sabine's triton and wrapped his tail around the top of the middle prong, standing tall like an extension of the triton. Sabine turned back to face The Kilk. She paused, then raced at him with her triton and The Kilk swam up and away from her. Sabine followed and they sprinted towards the surface of the ocean and surged out into the air.

Sabine and The Kilk pointed their weapons at each other. Electricity emanated from them, sparks buzzing, visible here in the open air, stirring up the whole sea. Rain began to fall and the wind appeared as if summoned from each corner of the earth, swelling the water into surface waves that reached high towards the sky and then crashed back down only to rise and fall again. All that could be heard was the roar of the ocean. Sabine kicked her tail hard and she shot up completely clear of the ocean in a powerful leap. The Kilk swirled the water with his staff and lifted himself up and out of the sea. They circled each other and smashed their triton and staff together and crashed back down, falling on their sides in opposite directions. The water splashed high above and over them, enclosing them in the sea once again.

Sabine came back to the surface but couldn't see The Kilk. She looked frantically over her shoulder, spinning on the spot. Then, up through the water he rose, arms spread wide, water dripping from him back into the sea. Sabine positioned her triton and pointed it at his throat. And then, the most unexpected thing happened. The Kilk stopped and stared at Jack, his eyes fixing upon the seahorse and seeming to stare into him. There was a softening in the Kilk's gaze, just a fraction, as if his soul had connected with Jack's. Jack, more than terrified, bravely held his gaze and looked back into The Kilk's eyes. It was the pause that Sabine needed.

She took hold of Emily, unwrapping her from her arm. Emily stiffened her flippers and stretched them out and Sabine reached her arm back to gather momentum – and then she hurled Emily like a boomerang towards The Kilk. Emily spun like a torpedo and delivered a blow to his head with her fins. Then, still spinning, she whirled around the back of his neck. Confused, he raised his hand and tried to grab her, but she continued spinning around him and towards his right hand. She seized his staff and returned to Sabine in one fluid circular motion. Sabine took the staff in her free hand and Emily wrapped herself back around Sabine's left forearm.

The Kilk was shocked but he quickly recovered and sent shots of balled-up sea spiders at Sabine. She used Emily's shield-like shell to protect herself and they bounced off Emily and rebounded back towards The Kilk.

Sabine, with the triton in one hand and the staff in the other, spread her arms wide and held her triton out, commanding the megalodon's tooth to come to her. It shook inside the sphere at the top of the Kilk's staff; slowly at first, then it started to tremble more violently. It shuddered and lurched forward, then stopped, pressed up against the strands of cartilage. Sabine carried on calling for the tooth, but it held tight, stuck inside the sphere. Emboldened by the exchange with The Kilk, Jack unwrapped his tail from the top of the triton, he stretched it out and glided the short distance to the spear and wrapped his tail around the twisted cartilage cage at the top of the staff. He leaned inside and nudged the tooth with his nose. It was big and sharp and the two edges were covered in tiny grooves. Jack kept going, nudging it until it shifted and turned onto its side at the edge of the cage. Jack gave it one last push and knocked it out into the beam of the triton's call. It came floating over to Sabine and she held it hovering in the water in front of her with her triton. Jack jumped out of the staff and Sabine dropped it, letting it fall away into the ocean. She reached out her left hand and the tooth fell into her palm. Sabine lifted it up, examining it for a brief moment. Then she threw it high in the air like a volleyball and, with her triton, sent it hurtling towards The Kilk. It pierced through his skin and straight into his stomach. He wailed and shrieked as his body spread out seeming to dissolve into the water. Then he dispersed and was gone.

The sea spiders scattered, camouflaging back into urchins and sinking down into the ocean. Emily unravelled from Sabine's arm and the trio floated gently on the surface of the water as the rain slowed to a calm shower.

'We did it!' Jack said, as he and Emily leapt towards each other and embraced, Emily wrapping her flippers around Jack and pulling him towards her. Then they let go and started bopping from side to side, mirroring each other's movements as they danced back and forth, swaying their heads and bodies in unison.

'I can't believe it!' Emily said.

'We took on a *sea demon*,' Jack said.

'And we *won*,' Emily said.

The two continued to jig together, Sabine watching

amused, but still anxious. Eli swam over and wrapped his tentacles around Sabine.

'Thank you, Sabine,' he said, and bowed his head.

Sabine bowed her head back and Eli let her go. 'You lost another tentacle,' she said, counting his remaining arms.

'Yes, but you should see the other guy,' Eli grinned at her. 'Esra's got *no* legs.'

Sabine smiled, 'What about the others?'

Eli faltered and said, 'They're ok.'

Sabine looked at him uncertain, but turned to her friends.

'When you two have finished high-fiving each other, shall we go and save Henry?'

'Henry!' Emily said, and the foursome turned and began the swim back to the shark net.

Chapter Ten

Share the Ocean

Sabine, Jack and Emily sped with Eli through the deadened world of the Mediterranean Sea.

'Where are the others?' Sabine asked Eli.

'We agreed we would meet back at the border where the net is. After I struck Esra, I came after you and went down through the ship to the tunnels,' Eli updated them. 'The dolphins drove the killer whale back. Sir Raynault fought and killed Kinslee.' Jack and Emily cheered. 'But then Deniella killed Sir Raynault.' The trio stopped in shock. 'So Lieutenant Howes killed Deniella.' Sabine put her hand to her mouth. 'We had a few losses in the battle but we won the war,' Eli said.

The group swam the rest of the way in silence. They reached the border by dusk and saw the shark net up ahead.

'Not much further,' Eli said as he adjusted course slightly to keep heading north-west towards the location where Henry was trapped. They were tired and hungry and looking forward to getting to the other side and out of this oppressive part of the ocean. They paused at the net and Jack swam over to it and anchored his tail inside one of the squares, looking through to the other side.

'Let's cross here,' Eli said and he slipped easily between

the squares in the net, pausing briefly as he made sure the gap was big enough to squeeze his eyes through. Sabine's two friends attached themselves to her and they swam up and leapt over in one quick, confident move. They travelled alongside the net, feeling exhausted as the events of the very long day started to catch up with them, until finally they could see Henry up ahead. Ava was still there with a group of her angel fish friends, buzzing uselessly around him where he lay, unmoving and traumatised.

Ava saw them approaching and swam over to Jack. 'I lost you, Jack. I'm so sorry,' Ava apologised.

Jack nodded, trying to accept the apology. He understood that she'd been in a panic but he wasn't quite ready to forgive her – the memory of being in Kinslee's mouth was still too fresh.

Sabine turned to all of the angel fish.

'We need all of you to help,' she told them, but the angel fish weren't listening. They swam in furious zig-zags.

'Listen!' Sabine waved her arms to get their attention. 'Everyone needs to lend a fin and work together to bite through the ropes. We need to organise ourselves and take different sections.'

Sabine began directing them and soon rows of angel fish were nuzzling and chewing, cutting into the netting. Slowly, the fabric started to fray in places. Henry made choking sounds, distressed. The rope around his head started to come apart and he half rolled out as if falling out of bed, but his tail was still trapped caught with so much rope wrapped around it that they couldn't chew through. Jack helped co-ordinate and re-directed the fish from Henry's head to his tail to join the other fish chewing there but it was no use.

'Use the triton,' Emily said.

Sabine looked down at the triton in her hand. She held it up and aimed it at the sections of net that wound tightly around Henry's tail. A tiny buzz of electricity shot out of the end and easily cut through the binding. Henry was free. But he was barely moving. Sabine put her arms around his middle and started swimming slowly, carrying him through the water and using her hands to direct water into his gills. They moved in and out, sucking in the water fast. He was dazed and confused and half dead. Sabine carried on carefully swimming with him, helping to revive him. Ava followed behind with Jack and Emily. Slowly, very slowly, Henry started to come back to life. Sabine kept going patiently. Suddenly, a weak voice came out of him.

'Thank you,' he said, sounding very hoarse.

'Of course,' she said.

'I'm sorry for what I said before.' His large black eyes rolled downwards in his hammer-shaped head to look away from her, embarrassed.

'I get it. You were scared,' Sabine said kindly.

Henry swivelled his eyes back to hers and they smiled at each other. They continued to swim together until Sabine reluctantly let Henry go, her arms spread out ready to catch him. But he swam gently by himself and turned back to her. Ava swam up and floated next to his head.

'Henry!' Ava placed her fins around one side of his big head and hugged him. Then she started gently pecking at his skin. 'I'm hungry,' she said.

'Me too,' Henry said and they swam off together to join his school of hammerhead sharks.

Marvin and Garvin appeared with Finn and Gibbons.

'Where's Toyah?' Jack asked him. 'Does she know about Sir Raynault?'

'She's with her family. She's doing ok,' Gibbons answered. 'You've done so well, Sabine. We are truly grateful.'

'In time, the ocean should restore itself and find its natural balance again,' Eli said.

'If only we could learn to share it,' Emily said. 'We take so much more than we need.'

'Fear, isn't it,' Eli said. 'The Kilk let his fear of sharks drive him. He was too busy thinking about his enemies instead of making friends.'

'The Kilk was a third-generation demon. He grew up hating sharks,' Finn told them.

'He has a seahorse in his mother's side of the family. It's why he paused when he saw Jack,' Eli said.

'It was a vital chance,' Sabine said.

'I knew I was required,' Jack grinned, bouncing around and doing a little jig again.

'Jack freed the tooth from the staff as well,' Emily informed them.

'Doubly required!' Sabine said.

'Well done, J-Em!' Marvin said. He and Garvin were back in their Hawaiian shirts, sunglasses in place – forever the coolest creatures in the ocean.

Gibbons came over, crossed his fins in front of him and bowed to Jack, who narrowed his eyes in suspicion. Then, choosing to believe that Gibbons was sincere, he bowed his head in return.

Gibbons turned to Sabine, 'Your father would be proud,' he said.

'So . . .' Eli turned to Sabine, '. . . are you ready to take his place?'

'Yes,' Sabine clutched her triton. 'I want to help save the oceans.'

'Awooohooo,' Garvin cried.

'Do you want to see the base for Scalewave?' Eli asked.

'There's a base?' Sabine asked, intrigued.

'Of course!' Eli said. 'It's where your father set up the system.' And off they went with the Sea Council members, Eli leading them away from the net and out into the North Atlantic Ocean.

They followed him to a massive rock formation in shallow

waters off the coast of the south of Portugal. Pillars of coral reached up from the seabed and stretched out to meet each other to form a large open space with two different entrances that allowed sunlight to filter in from both directions. There were big seashells, open wide, circling a massive piece of brilliant fire coral in the centre. In the corner was a small piece of rock with a dent in the base. There was life and activity all around. Fish were swimming everywhere, some zipping in and out of their homes, others were lazily dawdling along exploring the colourful sea flowers, whilst others still, pecked and playfully nipped at each other.

'This is your base,' Eli said. 'The centrepiece is the main relay station – your coral transmitter. It's the heart of Scalewave.'

'Rays hang here like leaves on trees, waiting to receive electronic messages from fish in distress,' Finn said.

'Other branching corals have been set up across the ocean as stations and rays hang there waiting to receive a message and then off they go to relay the message to the next nearest station.'

'This continues until it reaches you, Sabine,' Eli told her.

Sabine looked around, taking it all in.

'It all looks so familiar,' she said.

'Well, you lived here until you were seven,' Eli answered.

Sabine swam around, running her hands over the rough stones and ledges, feeling the wonder and excitement.

'The triton is made from the same material as the coral transmitter,' Eli said. Sabine touched the two together like a power base and they cracked together, electricity pulsing out.

'I can feel that,' Sabine laughed.

'That rock in the corner with the dent in it is where you can put your triton when you sleep at night,' Finn said. Sabine swam over to it and ran her hand over the small stand for her triton and looked around, grinning.

Over the next few days, the trio worked hard setting up their new home. They rearranged stones and pebbles, tidied up the seashells and hung up new strands of plaited seaweed over the two entrances. All manner of fish and sea creatures dropped by to welcome Sabine and her friends to their new home and celebrate the return of Scalewave. Stefan showed up and raked through the seabed creating welcoming patterns in the sand. Another fish, an electric green and orange rainbow wrasse called Mathieu told Sabine how much she looked like her mother. The emotion that had been rising and falling had nearly bubbled over. It was so strange to meet creatures who were so familiar with her and her parents, but it was exciting to get to know her family through the stories of the other fish.

Once things calmed down a little, they each picked a spot in the base that would be theirs. Sabine chose a ledge that jutted out next to where the triton's base was so that she was always within arm's reach of it. Emily selected a ridge near one of the natural archways for an easy exit to the surface. Jack set up his quarters in a corner where a small cluster of blue sea fan coral grew and where he could anchor himself at night. He was taking the longest to sort himself out. He had unpacked his jumpers and waistcoats onto a wrinkle in the rock next to the sea fan coral and hooked his rucksack to

one of its light blue branches. Now he was moving some pretty blue seashells around that seemed to hold onto the light and glow softly. Jack tried to nudge one into position with his nose but it would not roll over.

'It's too heavy,' Jack moaned, looking to Sabine.

'You can do it. You're a jack of all trades,' Sabine grinned.

'Don't jack it in,' Emily chimed in.

'Try jacking it up,' Sabine added.

'Or ask a jack fish for help,' Emily said.

'Don't be such a Jack-the-lad,' Sabine finished.

Jack floated, blinking at them, his face completely deadpan. Sabine and Emily curled their lips inwards, pressing them together, trying not to laugh. Jack then burst out laughing and Sabine and Emily joined in.

Toyah came racing into the cavern.

'Georgia, the great white shark, is on the move to Hawaii. She's ready to give birth!'

'Amazing!' Sabine clapped her hands.

'After 18 months of being pregnant, phew,' Emily said and wiped her brow with her torn left flipper.

'Is she moving to the birthing coastlines?' Sabine asked.

'Yes, but there's a cage of divers nearby throwing chum into the water,' Toyah said, rushing out her words.

'Chum?' Jack looked bewildered.

'It's where Land Creatures throw the blood and flesh of animals into the sea to attract sharks,' Emily answered.

'Oh no,' Jack said.

'We need to find out what's going on and protect

Georgia!' Sabine looked panicked as she thought about what could happen.

Jack grabbed his rucksack, which was already prepared and stocked up with jumpers and food, and leapt into Sabine's hair. Emily held out her wrist and snapped her bracelet to Sabine's.

Sabine turned to the young stingray and said, 'We're on our way . . .'

The End